RIVETINGLY GREAT STORIES VOLUME 2

CONNOR WHITELEY

Any questions about the book, rights licensing, or to contact the author, please email connorwhiteley@connorwhiteley.net

DEDICATION

Thank you to all my readers without you I couldn't do what I love.

INTRODUCTION

Contrast to popular belief, mystery is actually a remarkably flexible genre that can both be a genre in its own right (obviously) and a subgenre of tons of other main genres. As well as mystery can be a subplot, a main plot or a little writing device that helps to build the suspense of a story so the reader keeps reading.

That's why when I wanted to create these five volumes, I just knew I had to have a volume that combined science fiction and mystery. Also, I wanted to demonstrate that these two genres can be merged in different ways.

Personally, I do love mystery in most of its different forms. I love private investigators and women sleuths most of all, that's why I write the Bettie English Private Eye Mysteries and I love every single one of those books. I will definitely keep writing them because they are so much fun to write.

In addition, I love detective fiction too. It's why I write a lot of short stories in my Kendra Cold Case Detective Fiction series where she has to solve London's most impossible, toughest and most twisted cold cases. That gets really messed-up quickly but it is a blast to write.

And on occasion, I am well-known for writing what I term "not-cosy mysteries" that involve a little old lady in a village in the south of England so it uses the idea of a cosy. Yet these don't conform to the subgenre expectations (like extremely slow pacing) so I don't market them as cosy stories. These come in the form of my Jane

Smith Amateur Sleuth mysteries.

Therefore, as you can see mystery is a very wide and interesting genre that covers a lot of ground and can be written in different ways with different characters and have different feels.

That's what I want to show you in this volume with a science fiction twist.

Some of the brilliant, gripping stories in these pages include "Candy Detectives" about a detective chocolate bar investigating the murder of his ex-boyfriend in a candy world. This was originally published in the three time Hugo-Nominated Pulphouse Fiction Magazine.

That gives you a great taste of a science fiction mystery on the extreme scale as you're taken to a rich, vivid world made entirely of candy.

Another great set of stories come from the near future with "Future Baking" amongst others that hint at how crime might change in the next few decades and how detectives and other people will have to adapt to stop the evil criminals.

Then finally, I do love a good crime story because I like to imagine I would be good at committing crimes if I wasn't such a good person by bound laws and my own moral code. So I have to sadly settle for writing my dream crimes in fiction so please expect assassins, thefts and a whole bunch of other unputdownable crime stories with a science fiction twist.

There are twenty stories for you to enjoy in this volume so please enjoy following these fun detectives and criminals as they compete to solve or commit science fiction crimes.

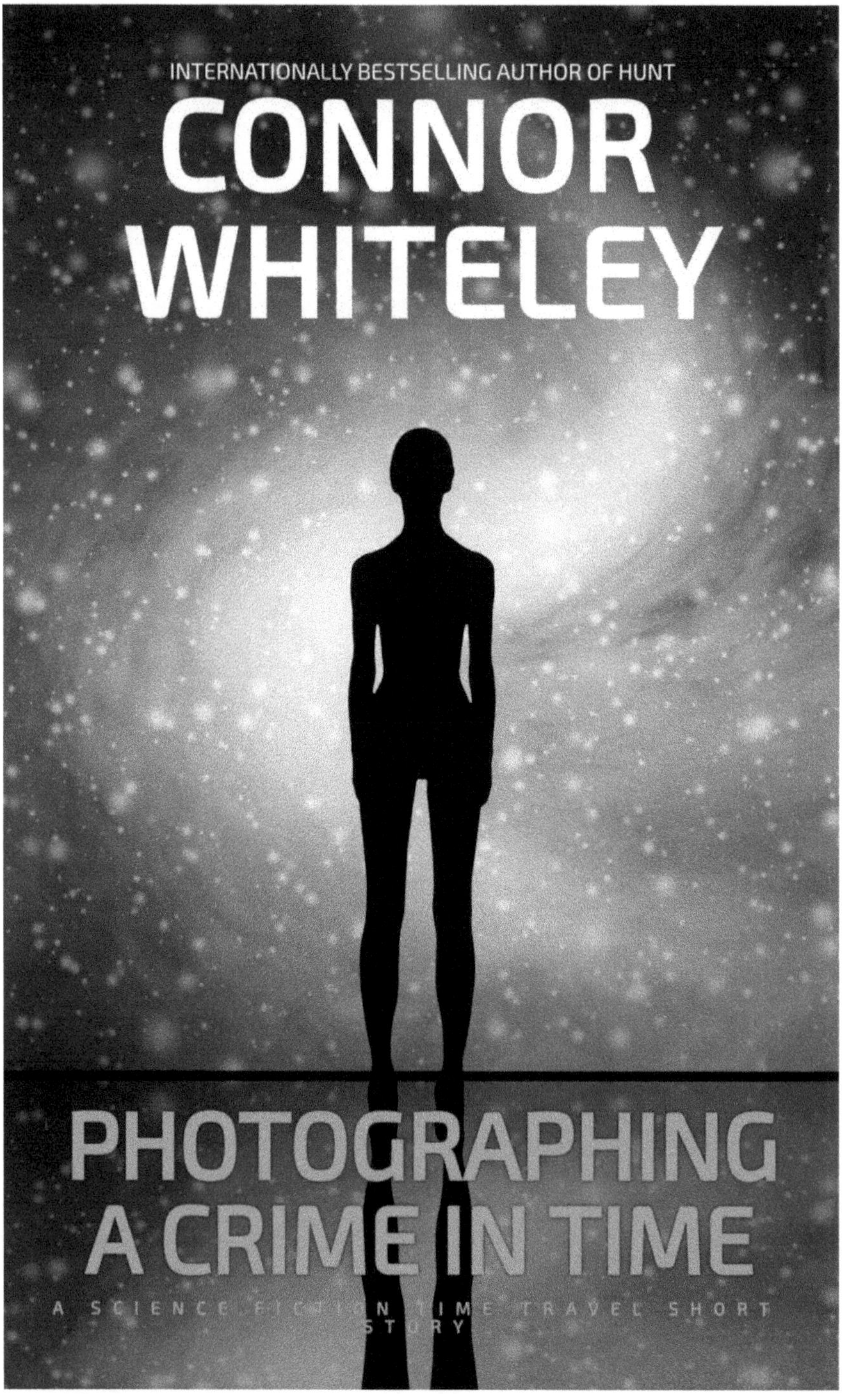
INTERNATIONALLY BESTSELLING AUTHOR OF HUNT
CONNOR
WHITELEY
PHOTOGRAPHING
A CRIME IN TIME

PHOTOGRAPHING A CRIME IN TIME

My name is Joanna Rusch and I have the extremely weird job of being a Time Photographer. Now you go ahead and laugh because I know that my job sounds so ridiculous, stupid and impossible. But please, let me assure you it is perfectly real and the consequences can be very, very real.

I have slipped in-between moments of time and photographed grand heroes of the past. Like Churchill, King Henry the Eighth and even Emperor Nero. Granted I seriously doubt some of those were actual heroes, but as my mummy always said 'morality doesn't pay the bills sweetheart'.

Of course she was right, that damn infuriating woman always was.

Until she died.

Which was why I became a Time Photographer because normally me and "my kind" travel into moments, take some pics and sell them to magazines. And most of the time for some serious cash, but I wanted to do a lot more good with my job.

So I wanted to take a picture of my mummy's killer.

As I stood in a massive cafe in the year 2030, I enjoyed staring at the rows upon rows of little metal tables with their holographic menus and metal chairs neatly tucked in around them.

The cafe walls were a rather wonderfully warm orange that I thought always gave it more of a Mexico compared to English feel, but that hardly made it a bad place. And even as I stood here I could taste the amazing chiles, stringy cheese and perfectly seasoned tacos on my tongue.

If I wasn't basically frozen in-between two moments of time

then I absolutely knew I would hear the joyous sounds of happy families and couples talking and laughing with a little gentle music playing in the background.

To be honest, I had been here so many times over the years that I just knew what everything was meant to be like. From the warm temperature to the calming family atmosphere to the brilliant staff that worked tirelessly each day.

I loved it here.

But considering I had read the police report tons of times over the decades, now I was here in the cafe at the moment my mother was dying. I was still rather surprised and... disturbed by it all.

You know, I was only a wee girl at the time when she was murdered, maybe 8 or 9 so now I was 45 with a husband and two kids of me own. It all seemed so strange actually being here.

I knew exactly where she died in here, the police report showed my beautiful mother with her loving eyes, long blond hair and massive caring smile spread out on the floor at the back like she had simply fallen. If it hadn't of been for the large stab wound thrusted into my mummy's heart, maybe, just maybe I would have lied to myself all these years and hoped that she had simply fallen back.

But the truth was different.

I felt my stomach twist as I realised what me being here actually meant. I was going to see what maybe I never should be able to see, at least the Time Code would keep me somewhat safe.

Due to this varied (and slightly pathetic) form of time travel meant I could literally only stay in-between two moments of time. Sure I could interact with the environment, like I could easily kick over the chairs, but when I left, time would start moving again and everything would reset itself.

Well, I say restarted. All I'm really doing is moving so slowly through this in-between of moments that time might as well as been stopped dead.

Ha. Yeah, maybe that wasn't the best thing to say right now.

I slowly started to walk through the cafe and I passed rows upon rows of families sitting at tables enjoying themselves and I honestly couldn't believe what I had read in the police reports.

Apparently no one had saw a thing except a man dressed in all black and his face was shrouded.

But now I was here, I couldn't believe it. There were so many people enjoying themselves, I couldn't understand why someone didn't see who killed my mummy.

Then I noticed the cafe sort of curved round to the left and... I saw it. I saw it all.

Maybe… no definitely. I should have prepared myself a lot more for seeing this, but right in front of me, I saw my beautiful loving mummy frozen in time as she looked like she was falling backwards, and the blood was already starting to drip out of the wound and into the soft fabric of her silk blouse.

My mummy always had made sure she looked great whenever she went out. Not in a pompous stupid kind of a way, but the sort of way how you know someone deserves respect, they've worked hard and they have a little bit of money because of all of that.

But as I stared at my mummy in her white silk blouse, black trousers and her screaming face falling backwards. I seriously couldn't believe what I was doing.

I felt my stomach tighten into a painful knot and I just knew I shouldn't be here. I should have had another Time Photographer do this, but I was just so arrogant and desperate and stupid that I really believed I could handle this.

Then I looked at the man in front of her.

Over the decades I had imagined what her killer looked like so often. When I was a wee girl, I had thought her killer would have scales, tentacles and massive slashing teeth. Of course that wasn't the case but as a little girl I had no other ideas.

Then when I was in my early adulthood I honestly thought the man would look like a deranged serial killer with crazy eyes, dirty teeth and a large knife in his hand. That was definitely the image that stuck in my mind all these years.

But now I was actually here. I could see that the police report was right all along. The man holding the knife with my mummy's blood shining in the light was six-feet-six wearing nothing but a black tracksuit, a black mask and black trainers.

It was nothing to go on and I could easily see why the case had turned as cold as it did. There was just nothing to go on.

Thankfully because I was in-between moments of time and I could interact with everything, I could finally take off the mask and take a picture of her killer.

I didn't know if I wanted to.

Well no, that is entirely right. Of course I wanted to, then I could simply hand the photo into the police and they would catch the criminal. They had done it before and tons of times since, that's actually how I got the idea for this in the first place. I read a magazine article on a Time Photographer that had done something for Jack The Ripper.

Yet now I was here, I wasn't sure if I wanted to experience what could happen afterwards.

The case had been cold for so long, my mother was so popular and the media frenzy had been bad enough back then. But if the killer was caught then everything would happen all over again.

And I would have to experience all the pain, agony and anguish, and I suppose my so-called step-brothers and sisters would have to get called in for the trial too.

It wasn't that I didn't like my so-called family, but they were from a different marriage that my dad did after she died. I hated that new mother (Georgia was the bitch's name) and I really, really hated how she tried to erase all memory of my mummy from me.

That was something I never forgave her for.

I just focused on the horrible killer and slowly reached for the black mask. My hands started to shake so badly that I wasn't sure they could do it.

Then my fingers brushed some of the cold fabric. My hand shot back.

I couldn't do this.

There would be so much chaos, agony and problems caused by this, if I actually revealed who the killer was my life would never be the same again. And I loved my current life, I loved travelling through Time taking photos, being a mother and being a wife.

I didn't want that to change, I had grown so use to not knowing that I was comfortable in the fact her killer would never be found.

I looked at my mother's screaming face again and I just felt so powerless. That was the problem with being in-between moments of time. Whatever I did here would just be reset and time would carry on as it had.

My mummy would still die.

So what was the point of all of this?

My mummy would still be as dead as a doornail, my life would be in chaos and my own family… I honestly don't know what they would be like. And that was all before I even started to wonder about my job, being a Time Photographer wasn't easy and I would need tons of time off to watch the trial, testify for how I got the photo and more.

I couldn't do that.

I slowly started to turn around when I saw a rather young man, probably 19, sitting at a table with some friends and he honestly looked like he was about to get up. The man had long brown hair, a concerned smile and his eyes… there was something so driven in those eyes.

Like he was going to help her.

I instantly knew who this man was, he had been the man who pressed my mummy's wounds until the paramedic's arrived, the man that had assured my mummy that I knew I was loved and most importantly this was the man I became best friends with.

Archie Long.

He had actually died a few weeks ago of a heart attack, but he had been so thrilled when I told him I was coming to do this little trip. He had wished me all the best, and how sorry he was that he couldn't do more for her that day.

I had to take the photo for him.

As I turned back round, I stretched out my hand and grabbed the cold fabric of the black mask, and I took it away.

My stomach felt like it would explode in agony as I stared at the face behind the mask.

It wasn't a man.

And to make matters a damn slight worse, I would always recognise that false evil smile, false blond hair and fake female nose. Because my daddy would later pay for all of these fakes to be redone with my mummy's money.

I was staring at Georgia. That selfish cold calculating bitch had killed my mummy to get my father.

I just raised my camera and I took tens of pictures from all different angles. I didn't want there to be any doubt about who this woman was.

This bitch of a step-mother was going to pay for what she did to me, my family and my mummy.

I was going to see her sent away for life.

***

About ten years later after all the investigations, the three trials and the chaos, I finally got my justice and as I stood there in the little café surrounded by all the metal tables, warm orange walls and people standing up in utter horror at the murder, I just smiled.

I could never visit the same in-between moments again so I had come to a few moments later as the entire café screamed and panicked and froze at the murder.

And I'm seriously grateful that I was in-between moments here, I didn't want to hear people screaming, crying and panicking. I certainly didn't want to smell the Mexican food too.

My husband (who was amazingly still with me) wondered why I bothered coming back after all the pain, chaos and other nonsense that the trial caused and I didn't really know.

At the time I supposed I just wanted to see my beautiful mother a final time, but now I know it was for a very different reason.

I slowly raised my camera and really smiled as I watched the frozen people react in horror to the murder, and I moved so those people were behind me and I just smiled.

I clicked the camera and took a wonderful selfie with me smiling in amongst the chaos and horror and disgust in the background, because I wasn't just a Time Photographer now.

Anyone could do that, but now I was a Time Photographer that specialised in photographing a crime in time, and if that meant I could provide closure for others. Then I knew I was going to be extremely, extremely happy with my life.

AUTHOR OF ACCLAIMED AGENTS OF THE EMPEROR SERIES
CONNOR WHITELEY
THE WAR INSPECTOR
A SCIENCE FICTION MYSTERY SHORT STORY

THE WAR INSPECTOR

When I was a teenager, so maybe in the early 2080s, in the very poor country of England, me and my classmates were always too damn excited when we had our *War History* classes because war really was meant to be a thing of the past. There were no bullets, guns or bombers being made and all the "old methods" of war as my teacher said really were things of the past.

Now at the time, that was just flat out amazing to me because my grandaddy, uncles and aunts had all been sent off to war and they had been exploded, blown up and ripped to shreds.

I really did love my family.

But if no more bullets, bombs and weapons were being made then no one, absolutely no one had to go through the same pain, agony and torment that I had to experience when the military turned up at my parents' door and explained what happened to their parents, my grandparents.

There was no more war.

However, even I have to admit that thirty years later that I was extremely stupid and to be honest, the rest of the world was rather stupid as well. War was like an organism meaning that it lived, thrived and it never ever wanted to die.

So war returned rather quickly in the 2090s.

That's where I come in.

As I stand on the icy cold charred, blackened ruins of a sandy plane in Northern Africa that stretches on for hundreds of miles, I pull my thick fur coat tighter around me because whatever myths people had about Africa in the past, it was always more than a frozen wasteland nowadays.

It was freezing.

The landscape was awful with its black charred sand coursing, swirling and twirling around me for as far as I could see. The black sand blew gently in a cold breeze that seriously had some bite on it, but I was more concerned about the sheer flatness of it all.

You see, I, Hellen Carter, am a War Inspector working for the United Nations and whilst all forms of war are illegal as hell nowadays ever since my adolescence. A lot of countries don't listen to the United Nations and because bullets, guns and bombs leave too much evidence behind. Countries use immense missiles these days.

That's what I'm looking for, any sign of evidence of these missiles.

I had only looked at pictures of this area a few days ago whilst I was getting prepared for this assignment. There were massive beautiful sand dunes, trees and lakes in small pockets and there were even settlements of great nomadic people living off the land.

I didn't see any of that now.

All I saw was an endless wasteland of black sand with tiny smouldering columns of black smoke rising up faintly into the crystal clear blue sky. That had to be the most unnerving part of all of this, but the black smoke left the aromas of charred flesh, bones and corpses in the air leaving the bitter aftertaste of death as it clung onto my tongue.

Back when my family were in warzones and fighting for the United Nations, they often said and wrote about how dark the sky was with smoke, soot and death so it actually turned a little darker no matter how bright the sun was trying to be.

That was actually the first piece of evidence that an Annihilator Missile had been used, the only missile still in existence.

"You there!" someone shouted behind me.

I pulled my large white rucksack a little tighter and I really hated to imagine what awful people had found me. I really hoped they weren't raiders or something.

I turned around and was rather annoyed at myself for not detecting the large group of men and women in charred dirty clothes sneak up behind me. These certainly weren't locals with their modern western jeans, shirt and hiking boots.

These were most likely the war criminals that had launched the attack.

A rather tall woman slowly stepped forward and she didn't seem evil with her long blond hair, smooth skin and long slim legs (she was very hot I have to admit) but it was her grin that concerned me.

Then all of them got out their longswords that shone bright in the sunlight and almost blinded me.

I only just noticed that the peaceful howl of the wind that I had tuned out as mere background noise had stopped, and now I was alone in silence with these criminals.

"She's from the UN," the leader woman said. "If the UN sent her then they know what we're up to, so we have to deal with her and convert her,"

I took a few steps back. I had no idea who these people were but they were strange extremists for sure.

Annihilator missiles might have been extremely rare, having the power to turn entire small nations into nothing but blackened wastelands but very few countries had them. What was left of the US had some, the United European Nations had tons, China had a few more and the powerhouse of the Japanese Empire had a good chunk too.

I didn't think any of these people belonged to those nations but I think it was fair to say I was getting kidnapped by people who weren't my target. So war criminals were still free and these idiots were stopping me in my work.

"I'm not going anywhere with you criminals. I was sent by the UN to investigate the use of this missile and I have to keep the world safe. You cannot stop me," I said, very stupidly.

The group laughed at me just like how my childhood bullies did a lot of the time.

The leader woman came up to me and pressed her sword against my throat. "I think you will do exactly as we say because I agree with you. I do want to know who killed my family and you're going to help me do it,"

As much as I didn't want to admit it, I was rather intrigued because if these people were from this country then why didn't they die in the attack like their families?

That answer actually scared me a lot more than I ever wanted to admit. Even to myself.

***

"Greetings War Inspector,"

I have to admit that I've been working for the United Nations since I was 16 years old so a good thirty years, I've worked with national security services, international ones and I have in fact worked with a handful of criminal organisations as informants (and sex partners too) but these criminals were just fascinating.

They led me into a large yellow canvas tent after a five hour drive through the blackened wasteland towards their encampment that was very well established considering the attack.

The camp was impressive with its sweet-smelling flowers, freshwater spring and the stunning aroma of freshly roasted beef filled the air. The entire camp smelt like heaven and I loved it. I was also rather surprised to see so many people of so many nationalities, there were French, Chilian, Spanish and tons of others.

But there was no one from Africa here, there were Europeans, Americans and others. It made no sense, what could possibly bring all these people together?

The tent itself they led me to was very fancy with a large holographic table in the middle that showed a map of northern Africa with a red dot for where we were and they highlighted the blackened wasteland.

It easily covered all of northern Africa, this was a very high-powered Annihilator missile that basically took out half a continent.

The tent canvas walls were smooth, surprisingly clean and there were no other pieces of technology in here. I presumed this was a type of headquarters so I expected radios, communication devices and weaponry (illegal ones of course) but there was none of that.

Then I realised that only moments before a woman had said something to me and I smiled when I saw an old friend of mine, a Commander Victoria Grayson, was standing in the corner smiling at me.

I immediately went over and hugged her. It was great to see her again in her tan-coloured desert clothes after we served together in the middle east investigating acts of war there.

"What is this place?" I asked, forcing my excitement to remind in check. She was also sensational in bed.

"This is the United Nations Peace Division or what's left of it," she said.

I nodded. The UNPD was destroyed about two weeks ago when it was sent into Northern Africa to help defend the local population from the aggression of a Chinese, Russian and Korean alliance (for what all that would do). No one had heard anything for weeks, so why didn't Victoria respond?

"No communication devices," Victoria said, clearly knowing me way too well.

"I see. Well the UN knows something is off and they want me to find evidence of a war crime here,"

Victoria just laughed and I had really missed that beautiful smile and her perfect teeth. I knew why she was laughing because "Act of War" seems like an understatement when half a continent had been shattered and blackened and scorched.

I went over to the holographic table, Victoria thankfully joined me.

"Me and my forces were in the southern end of Africa hunting down a drug lord when the attack happened. We raced back but there were soldiers that forced us back here so we couldn't investigate,"

Victoria said.

I frowned. I hated the idea of there being so many soldiers on the ground and a country had to be behind this because I couldn't imagine terrorists or people without state funding, getting their hands on an Annihilator missile for one, but also having the manpower to launch the attack and then launch ground forces as soon as they were able to.

Something much, much larger was going on here and I didn't like that.

"I presume your forces tracked the soldiers back to their base?" I asked, knowing Victoria was way too good not to do just that.

She shook her head. "We tried but there was a sniper that picked off our forces one by one,"

"Damn it," I said but in all fairness that might be what actually saved us.

"What you thinking?" Victoria asked.

"I know an annihilator missile levels the ground making it perfect to see enemy forces incoming but I know that a sniper has to shoot from a single location. Is it possible to triangulate the sniper's position using the positions of your dead soldiers?"

Victoria slowly nodded because I knew that she was too smart not to see what I was saying, and it was standard military protocol that whenever a soldier died their body's coordinates would be logged and stored.

Victoria went over to the holographic map of North Africa and bought up the location of the bodies. She then ran a computer programme to find the position of the sniper.

"Too many shooters. Maybe three different snipers," she said.

I grinned. "What were the positions of the snipers?"

She ran another programme and I just smiled as it showed us that the three snipers were spaced equally around a large black square.

She bought up satellite images and it was next to impossible to see because of the advance anti-thermal imaging technology and the canvas of the tents were black like the sand. But I could have sworn this was a military camp.

Probably by the exact same soldiers that had attacked Victoria's forces earlier.

I took out a small phone from my rucksack and I dialled my boss in New York. We needed military support immediately and I wanted answers.

I had to find out who the hell was behind this most horrific attack.

***

The wind blew through my long black hair as I wrapped my arms around Victoria's wonderful thin waist as we zoomed towards the enemy encampment on our hoverbikes.

The roar of other hoverbikes, hover-trucks and helicopters was deafening and the smell of damp from the hydrogen fuel was wonderful.

I was more than glad to have my two pistols on my waist and a machine gun (UN authorised of course) on my back just in case things turned violent.

Up ahead immense black tents flapped in the breeze and then bullets screamed through the air.

These were certainly the terrorists and criminals.

A hoverbike exploded next to me.

Victoria went faster.

Everyone did.

Everyone constantly swerved to make them impossible to shoot clearly.

Helicopters shattered like glass.

Flaming wreckage rained down upon us.

People screamed. Their bodies exploded.

Me and Victoria went faster.

Rockets roared through the air.

Smashing into whatever they hit.

We were getting slaughtered.

Me and Vic went faster.

We were nearing the camp.

A bullet smashed into our bike.

Our bike popped.

Steering out of control.

Vic leapt off.

I followed.

I smashed into the dark black sand of the wasteland and I heard heavy military boots pound the ground towards us.

I leapt up.

Whipping out my pistols. I wasn't dying here.

I aimed my pistols at the incoming white uniformed troops and I fired.

My bullets ripped through their flesh.

Chests exploded.

Heads gapped with holes.

I charged at them.

The soldiers were so confused.

I kept firing.

Vic joined me.

The soldiers snapped out of their confusion.

They fired back.

I rolled across the sand.

Shooting as I went.

I leapt into the air.

Firing wildly.

The enemy screamed.

A whip slashed at my back.

I screamed.

The whip wrapped around my ankle.

Victoria screamed.

I smashed onto the ground and just shook my head as I watched as a large American man pulled me over to him. He was fat, badly dressed and had such a foul evil grin on his face like I was nothing more than even a mere plaything.

He dragged Victoria over too, I was just glad I still had my machine gun on my back but it was stabbing me too and I couldn't reach it with this man so close to me.

"Impressive that you have killed all my men and women. That is most impressive for you European scum," he said.

"Now I remember why America launched annihilator missiles at itself. Remind me, how many missiles did the South launch at the North and vice-versa?"

The man frowned. "America survives,"

I didn't really doubt that too much because the leadership of the North and South parties in America probably "saved" a bunch of people in bunkers or something. But I suppose that other missiles must have survived the destruction of the US.

"Why Northern Africa?" I asked, focusing on the whip in his left hand.

I didn't know how but I just had to loosen the whip just enough so I could jump up, get away from it and use my machine gun.

I just had to.

"Because everything bad in the world can be traced back to Africa,"

I didn't actually have the heart to tell him that all of humanity was from Africa so he was calling himself bad (which he was) but I noticed that his left hand loosened on the whip whenever he got annoyed.

"You are stupid though because what about Southern Africa? What about all those black people that you hate? The United Nations will allow them to invade the US now,"

Of course there would be no invasion at all but he didn't know that ever since the US destroyed itself it wasn't allowed in the UN.

The man frowned. "What! Those-"

As the stupid man started using a ton of very racist and foul language to describe innocent people I tuned it out and my entire body relaxed I watched him get angrier and angrier.

He finally released the whip.

I rolled backwards.

I leapt up.

I whipped out my machine gun.

And I fired!

The man screamed and his eyes widened as the tens upon tens of bullets smashed into him.

I didn't care about this man so I simply went over to Victoria and it was only now I realised that the whip had wrapped around her arms and legs so that's why she couldn't help me.

But at least I now had my answers and I needed to urgently report to the UN.

***

After another day where I oversaw the UN's security forces investigating the encampment properly, searching laptops, examining bodies and interrogating a prisoner that the Americans had, I had finally been able to write my report and now that it was a week later, I was finally listening to the wonderful UN discussing what they were going to do.

Since I wasn't an official representative of a UN member state, I was only allowed to stand in the Viewing Gallery, a rather posh stuck-up name for a very high glass box that allowed me to stare down below where the UN council chamber was.

The immense golden handcrafted chairs that the representatives sat on looked stunning and the freshly polished brown flooring only made the chamber below even more alluring and the raised golden stage and seats tens of metres into the air was breathtaking.

The bright white lights of the chamber perfectly illuminated everyone and there was a great mix of rich and poor, fat and slim and old and young people in the chamber today. All wearing their white robes of office.

And I was shocked that I could smell the "official" perfume of the UN, a very rich sweet-smelling mixture of flora from all seven continents. It actually smelt amazing but normally no one wore it.

That was how important everyone believed this moment to be, and it truly was.

The President of the UN was an elderly woman of Scottish descent and she had already assassinated some pathetic arguments from the US representatives (I still don't know why they were given emergency permission to come here even though they weren't a member state) and her long wavy grey hair made her look imposing, scary and a force to be reckoned with.

Even I was surprised at the sheer amount of representatives that had turned up today, the entire chamber was full and believe me, that flat out never happened. But every single member state wanted to help pass judgment on the US for annihilating (and murdering) so many billions of innocent people.

Some people were proposing that the US shouldn't be punished because it was a nation now ruled by terrorists and self-fish groups and I could understand that. Others were calling for the US to be controlled by the UN directly. I could also understand that.

But my proposal had been the simplest and a lot of members liked it, I honestly didn't care about what the US did behind closed doors. The remnants of the North and South could continue to bomb each other as far as I cared but I didn't want them hurting anyone else.

So I was calling for every single square inch of the US's remaining territory to be searched and *all* weapons (including annihilator missiles) had to be taken away. It didn't matter if the weapon was an artifact, antique or family heirloom, it had to be taken and I wanted to personally oversee the destruction of the weapons afterwards.

Everyone was in fairly strong agreement with me.

But hey, what do I know I'm only a War Inspector, not an official representative. And yes I am still annoyed I have to stand up here alone.

"Hello stranger," Victoria said as she came onto the glass platform wearing a very sexy baby blue dress and holding two mugs of piping hot mint tea.

It was great she remembered it was my favourite drink as she passed me a mug.

"You think they'll go into the US?" Victoria asked.

I just smiled. Because I was always surrounded by the UN's politics, I knew exactly how they worked and sometimes even I forget that others like Victoria weren't as familiar. To me the UN was my world, but I suppose Victoria thought the same about the military.

"They will. England and some of the other forgotten nations of the world will just like to drag this debate out so people can remember they still exist," I said.

Victoria laughed. Damn, I had forgotten how beautiful her laughter was.

I went over to her and playfully knocked into her. "You know, if they do pass my proposal I will need military backup. I would need to appoint a commander, if you want to spend some more time with me,"

Victoria shrugged grinning. "Well, I do hear Asia has some great drug lords I could hunt down instead. I'm not sure what America could offer me?"

I kissed her on the cheek, savouring the great taste of her smooth skin. "There's plenty more where that came from,"

Victoria shrugged. "Well Hellen, you might have yourself a deal there,"

And as she winked at me, I heard the President of the UN stand up and I didn't even look at the President as she announced the result.

"Peace has come home," the President said.

I simply nodded as I knew my proposal had passed and at least my beautiful Victoria wouldn't be leaving me any time soon, and maybe we could develop whatever we had started in the middle east further. I had no idea if what we had was love or not, but I was really, really excited to find out.

And I had no idea that it had taken an Annihilator missile to bring me, The War Inspector, together with a beautiful woman. It was a strange, magical and wonderful way to start the next chapter of my life but I was more than excited about finding out what happened next.

AUTHOR OF BETTIE ENGLISH PRIVATE EYE MYSTERIES
CONNOR WHITELEY
TO STOP OR BE DAMNED
A MYSTERY SHORT STORY

TO STOP OR BE DAMNED

19th November 2100

London, England

Financial Investigator Ella Fox absolutely loved her job investigating the super rich, the super corrupt and the various international terrorist organisations that had decided that poor old lonely England was the perfect place to stash their millions away.

She had to admit that the job had seriously changed in the past few decades but she still flat out loved it. Back when she first started in the 2040s, she mainly focused on the rogue elements of terror groups but now it seemed that she had to investigate entire terrorist nations and stop their money from funding international terrorism.

That was why she was having one of the most important meetings of her little life.

Ella wrapped her hands around the piping hot holographic mug of coffee as she leant against the white crystal railings of her top floor office, allowing her to admire all of London. She really liked watching the streams upon streams of pod-like flying cars rush and zoom about.

She had never got a flying car herself because she just didn't need it with her job, but she loved watching them cover the sky like a thousand arrows flying towards their target. Yet Ella's favourite part about the flying cars had to be that they made London a perfectly safe place to walk regardless of the time of day.

It was a walker's idea of heaven.

The River Thames was rather quiet today for a change with only a couple of old-fashioned cargo container ships bobbing along and the rest of the modern hover-ships were coming ahead into the various business districts of London.

It was beautiful.

The sweet aromas of watermelon, pineapple and grapefruit made Ella smile as the refreshing taste of holidays in the Caribbean with her family formed on her tongue. She had loved those days, it was just a shame most of her family had died in the English-Russo war just before Russia collapsed and was absorbed into the Chinese Empire.

The vibrating of the lift behind her made her look away from the beautiful view and she folded her arms as the blue holo-doors of the magnetic elevator opened and her boss appeared.

She had a lot of respect for Inspector Francis Drake. He always looked hot and wonderful in his tight-fitting navy suit, black shoes and expensive pocket watch (that did make him look like a bit of dick too) but she didn't like having meetings with him.

Especially about her work because everyone knew he only invited you to a private meeting for two reasons. Either your work was so amazing that he wanted to personally thank you and gift you some of the seized money as a bonus. Or he was going to tell you to stop in the interest of National Security.

Ella really doubted it was going to be the first, because her current case about investigating the money of terrorists was nothing short of what she normally did.

And he had never thanked her for that before.

"Ella," Francis said, "thank you so much for agreeing to my request,"

A small magnetic door opened next to Ella and then she followed Francis inside to his office.

She had never been in his office before and she was amazed. There wasn't a single sheet, wall or anything made of metal. It was all seamlessly made from glass, crystal and holograms that crackled ever so slightly. It was so beautiful and impressive.

Ella went over to the hovering desk and when Francis offered her a seat she refused.

"Please update me on your investigation," Francis said, but Ella already knew he was only being polite.

"I've been investigating the terrorist group known as Chai La for the past four months. They're a small band of Chinese special Forces that focus on breaking down governments, creating civil unrest and then convincing people to overthrow their countries,"

"Allowing the Chinese Empire to sweep in, save the day and then create puppet governments," Francis said.

Ella nodded. "Exactly. Chai La isn't connected to anything official in the Empire but from information from the EU, Aussie Empire and what's left of the US I've managed to understand that Chai La was moving money into England,"

Francis shook his head.

"The information is all there and I have managed to track down over two thousand accounts connected to Chai La. These accounts are being used to fund international terrorism including the assassination of the EU President four years ago,"

Francis sat up perfectly straight and Ella just smiled. It was always nice to see Francis panic a little.

"I wonder what would the EU do if they learnt it was English money that funded the assassination?" Ella asked wanting to stress Francis even more.

"Nothing," Francis said. "Because I am shutting down your investigation immediately,"

"What!" Ella shouted. "I have found billions of pounds in Chai La bank accounts that are being used to support terrorism. Why would the English Government want us to stop investigating?"

Ella really didn't understand this because she was just doing her job to try and save lives and make the world a safer place.

"Wake up woman and get a grip on reality," Francis said knowing she didn't understand. "England seems the billions to support our economy. Ever since Scotland and Wales gained independence and Ireland was reunited, England has been struggling with our economy,"

Ella laughed. "So what? Then surely we do the intelligent thing and rejoin the EU like Wales and Scotland. Their economies are far better than yours and their population is a tenth of the English,"

"Never," Francis said like the very suggestion was acidic on his tongue. "England is a powerful country but we rely on those billions to fund and prop up the economy,"

Ella couldn't believe this was actually happening but she was never ever going to allow this to stand. This was wrong, corrupt and she wouldn't allow that billions not to be seized.

"And if we sanction Chai La," Francis said clearly not impressed with his own words. "Then we send a signal to the entire criminal underworld that England isn't a safe place for investing in. And yes we really are that desperate,"

Ella went over to Francis. "All the other money that I've ordered to be sanctioned over the decades. What happened to it?"

"It went back to the organisations it needed to go to with a hefty cut taken out of it,"

"Fuck you," Ella said. "We have to stop them or be damned by helping them."

She was so damn angry that she had spent decades of her life claiming to investigate the finances of the corrupt just to have that corrupt money that was killing innocent people to be handed back to the bastards.

This was evil, immoral and she couldn't believe how horrific this was.

"Last question," Ella said seriously hating her boss. "That bank account that funded the assassination of the EU leader. Did England give the terrorist the sanctioned money?"

"Of course it was. England gave it to the terrorists knowing all about their plan," Francis said knowing she hated him. "And you know what I don't doubt the English Government would do it again,"

Ella nodded. This was the very last thing she had ever wanted to hear but it was good news in a way. She now had power, leverage and influence to use against the English Government whenever she needed it.

And she was more than determined to find a way to sanction Chai La's bank accounts. She couldn't live with herself if she didn't try everything in her power to stop those terrorists from using their money to kill innocent people.

"This isn't over," Ella said as she stormed out the office.

And she already knew that a million eyes, ears and intelligence officers were watching her like a hawk.

***

The next day Ella wasn't too surprised to see that there were at least ten badly dressed intelligence officers in their black suits watching her as she went down a long narrow London street on her way to work. She had wanted to contact the EU and Americans from inside work so she could be arrested for treason or some rubbish, but now she didn't doubt Francis had already destroyed all the evidence of the accounts.

And she seriously wouldn't have been surprised if the English Government had actually contacted Chai La and warned them about her.

That was all part of her plan.

Ella smiled as she got out into a massive London street in Old Town that still had the horrible bright white stone houses from the early 21st century. The houses were narrow, small and cramped, and she still had no idea why anyone would want to live in some small places but that was life.

There were no cars or black cabs on the road, it was empty and that meant there was no place for anyone to hide.

Again that was what she wanted. Because she didn't doubt for a second that the English weren't the only people looking at her. She had already noticed one or two Asian men looking at her this morning and she didn't doubt the Americans and Europeans weren't far behind.

Ella went into the middle of the street and simply stood there and as all ten of the English intelligence officers came out the narrow road and looked at her. They scanned the area but this wasn't a trap.

Ella subtlety made sure her holo-phone had its recording and livestream features working and then she made sure it was transmitting to all the best media outlets.

All the intelligence officers took out their guns and three Asian men joined the English officers.

"This isn't exactly what I expected," Ella said meaning every word of it. "I expected the English to try and kill me but I didn't expect Chai La to come in person"

The Asian men grinned with their horrible yellow and blackened teeth on full display.

"The Empire is growing," one of the English men said but they all looked the same to Ella. "The EU and Aussie Empire are growing stronger with each passing day. Even the US is growing stronger after they nuked themselves,"

Ella nodded because she could finally understand what was happening here. "The English Government wants to join the Empire,"

Everyone but Ella laughed like she was the dumbest person on Earth.

"The English Government are clueless so Chai La will create chaos, make the people see reason and then the Government will fall,"

"And the Empire will rise in its place," Ella said knowing exactly how Chai La operated. She had seen it time and time before in the Indo-Pacific regions, Africa and even South America was starting to turn towards the Chinese Empire.

But thankfully the Aussie Empire was growing in power in South America too.

All the intelligence officers took a few steps towards Ella with their guns firmly aimed at her chest.

Ella really wished she had a bulletproof vest or something but she was an investigator. Not a soldier, she didn't know how she would even get one.

"Is Francis a member?" Ella asked.

The Asian men nodded. "Of course. He sanctions terror groups and he gives the money to us after he gives some to the Government to keep them happy,"

"The Government knows what Francis is doing," another one said. "They don't care so you need to stop this,"

Ella looked around to check if she could escape but she noticed there were three other Asian men at the end of the road cutting her off.

And it wasn't like she could outrun bullets.

The three Asian men in front of her went over to Ella and stuck their guns on her forehead.

"You are going to die now and then no one will remember you or your name. And soon the English will only know the word Chai La as the heroes that saved them,"

Ella laughed. "Then you are deluded because do you really think France would allow the Chinese Empire to get a country so close to its borders?"

Ella loved it as the Asian men's eyes widened in sheer horror and she really hoped the Europeans were here now.

But nothing happened.

"Nice try," someone said.

A gunshot went off.

An Asian's head exploded.

Ella leapt to one side.

More gunshots went off.

Heads exploded.

Chests boiled.

Searing brain matter splattered everywhere.

Ella recognised the weaponry. It was European Laser snipers.

After a few moments Ella stood up and she gasped as she saw fifteen bodies charred, smouldering and cooked alive scattered around her. The air was choking with the aroma of cooked flesh but it was a sheer nightmare.

Then Ella heard five sets of heavy military boots storm towards her.

Ella looked up at the five women from French Special Forces as they came towards her scanning the area as they went to make sure there were no more Chai La members. There wasn't.

"Miss Ella," one woman said. "You need to come with us immediately. The EU President requests an audience with you about your investigation and in exchange, we'll help you blow the lid off this corruption so England can never become part of the Empire,"

Ella smiled at them. That did sound nice but she did have a condition.

"But I have to oversee what happens to the money after it's sanctioned," Ella said.

The women nodded and Ella knew it was the best she was going to get because they probably didn't have the power to meet her demand anyway.

Ella went off with them anyway because she had to make sure Chai La was stopped, the world was safer and she had to make sure that the money couldn't be used to steal any more innocent lives.

***

Ella absolutely had to admit as she laid down on the massive Queen-sized bed of her brand-new Parisian apartment made with the finest black silk sheets money could buy. Ella had to admit the past week had been a lot of fun.

The women had escorted her to France and then Brussels immediately, she had met the EU President (great woman) and they had agreed that Chai La had to be stopped. And because Ella was rather surprised by how great her memory was about the bank accounts she had managed to recover all the bank account numbers within two days.

All because she remembered how she had uncovered the web of secret accounts in the first place. She had flat out loved working with the Europeans on the case because they were so joyous, fun and they loved a good laugh.

After the accounts were found, the EU President contacted the English Prime Minister to make them sanction the accounts and transfer the money over to the EU. Ella was hardly surprised that they refused but after the EU promised to drop a few trade sanctions they caved, how English of them.

Ella had no idea how she was going to use the terrorist money, she had kept a million for herself because she was now an EU citizen working for the French as a financial investigator. But the rest of the money she was more than determined to invest in the communities that needed it most.

She would set up new schools, new reading programmes and new soup kitchens and just make sure that the money was used to help innocent people. Because that was actually her job, she might have investigated terrorists and the corrupt but her real job was to help the innocent people that relied on her investigations.

And that was why she would always stop terrorists and she would never be damned by letting them continue to fund terrorism and kill them.

That wasn't who she was and it was never who she was going to be.

AUTHOR OF BETTIE ENGLISH PRIVATE EYE MYSTERIES
CONNOR WHITELEY
CANDY
DETECTIVES
A CANDY SCIENCE FICTION MYSTERY SHORT STORY

CANDY DETECTIVES

The world of flesh and blood is no more.

When the climate crisis got too much, fires engulfed the world, floods engulfed the coast and the world was on the brink of war over the dying resources. Someone created a solution.

People hated it. They really, really did. But they knew it was all their fault so they couldn't moan too much.

Overnight the world leaders unleashed a massive wave and when people woke up the next morning, they were flesh and blood no more.

They were candy.

At first it was just plain weird, everyone awoke to become their favourite type of candy and even the houses, roads and everything else was made of a candy or another.

But it was delicious.

And at least the climate crisis was basically over with humans stopping producing as much fuel fossils and power. (Believe me, candy people hate heat!) Then the over-farming of cows and fish stopped too, candy don't eat meat thankfully.

I thankfully became my favourite candy of them all, I loved it, I became a toffee person and I was delicious! I quickly discovered that when I decided to eat a bit of myself and it grew back. I grow back!

That was amazing.

But I'd be lying if I didn't say it made my job more interesting as a detective, it seems some people didn't lose their sweet tooth and people loved to eat other candy people.

Which lead me to this case.

Feeling the beating hot sun warm up my soft delicious toffee skin, I tried to ignore the brown droplets of toffee sweat dripping down my back as I focused on the crime scene around me.

The suburbs were a lot further out than I normally travel but when a candy killer is on the loose, I have to hunt them down. It's just who I am.

As I looked at each of the ten ginger houses that lined the street, I smiled at each of their icing decorations and the chocolate buttons that made up the roof tiles. I even almost laughed at one of the houses on the end, needless to say someone had eaten the roof. I know the feeling all too well.

The sweet chocolatey smell in the air was amazing and it made me realise I don't miss my human life in the slightest, I always hated the disgusting smell of cars, fuels and fires. But these days the worse smell I get is when I come across some melted Haribos in the street.

I was about to return my attention to the crime scene but I heard the wonderful high-pitch laughing of hard boiled candy children. I looked around for them as seeing children happy and playing was a great way to deal with the horror of my job. But there weren't any, not a single child around, nor adult.

Odd.

As I turned my attention back to what I was meant to be doing, I stared down on the soft vanilla ice cream road (ignoring the pink candyfloss pathways) which had massive streaks of chocolate bars in it. I had to admit these days I certainly get more interesting crime scenes, some people had said that a chocolate bar had been murdered here but I needed a closer look first.

Feeling the soft ice cream melt and move under my soft toffee feet, I knelt down and loved the feeling of the ice cream chilling my knees slightly. I placed a finger in the chocolate mixture and nodded as I felt some electrical power run up my arm.

This was definitely a person, a candy person.

I have no idea who first discovered that died, melted or hacked up candies had a certain energy about them but I'm glad they did.

After the Candy Awakening, I was sick to death with all the prank calls when people had chopped up leftover candy bars and said someone was murdered. But there was no way to tell if it was a person or just a candy bar from the Old Times. I'm happy there's a way now.

My eyes narrowed on the chocolate mess as I noticed some

pieces were still solid and chunky, like in chocolate chip cookies. I didn't understand that because if the chocolate bar had been murdered and hacked up then all of him or her should be melted.

But they weren't.

The sound of splashing footsteps made me smile as I looked up to see a rather terrifying red gummy bear walk towards me. I say terrifying because, well, my human side still couldn't understand gummy bears walking around and doing things. It sounded like something from a children's horror film.

The gummy bear stopped and waved one of its paws at me, I nodded to my detective partner, *Frank*. (But between you and me, I'm really glad gummy bears can't talk because Frank was such a talker before the Awakening. If verbal diarrhoea was a condition, he would have had it)

Frank pointed towards the chocolate mess and whirled his gummy hands in front of his mouth, I knew he wanted me to explain it to him but I didn't know what to tell him.

I had to try. "Frankie boy, I donna what happened here. Seems some chocolate bar got killed. Some melted, some chunks,"

Frank stared at me. I guessed he wanted more but the Caramel Crime Scene Techs weren't done yet. I looked past Frank to see them scooping through the ice cream at the end of the Suburban street, maybe they were looking for more chocolate fragments, I don't know.

Frank pointed to some of the chocolate chunks and waved me over to look at them. I rolled my eyes and I knelt down next to him as I poked the chunks.

My eyes widened a little when I noticed these chunks were a different chocolate all together. I hadn't noticed it before but the victim was made from milk chocolate, very cheap and very cheap tasting. But these chocolate chunks, I don't know, maybe Belgium Chocolate.

Of course the only real way to tell would be to have the Caramel Techs test it but if there was a chocolate killer on the loose, we didn't have time for such things.

Frank looked at me with his massive (terrifying) gummy bear eyes. I instantly knew he wanted me to let me try some but that was unethical, probably illegal.

I could feel Frank stare at me whilst I looked at the rest of the chocolate melt away under the hot sun, but there were still large chunks of the victim. I still didn't understand it.

"Frankie boy, how come this Vic didn't all melt?" I asked.

I turned back to Frank and saw him pointing at the sun.

"No Frankie, the sun didn't melt our Vic but…" I said, as I understood what he meant and I stopped. I couldn't really believe it, could someone have melted our victim?

Looking back at the swirls of chocolate mess that were mixing into the ice cream, I nodded as I knew it was true. Some candy person must have melted the chocolate bar and these chocolate chunks were the burnt bits that wouldn't melt.

Clever, evil but clever.

Frank nodded as he knew I understood what he wanted. After a few moments, my chocolate phone pinged as I got a message from my Caramel Crime Scene Techs (I don't know why they didn't just walk over to us), they found the victim's ID and I knew the name.

Michael Vincent.

Of course to most of the Candy World it was just another name of a Chocolate bar but to me it was a special name. A great name belonging to an even greater man, the first man I'd ever loved.

I had to stand up and take a few steps back from the chocolate mess as I remembered how the beautiful human had helped me when my parents threw me out (and tried to kill me) for being gay. He helped me and he was a great man.

Just the idea of someone killing him made me tense and the little droplets of toffee sweat got larger. But I did have to smile at him becoming a chocolate bar, it was sort of an irony because he hated chocolate and a fitness freak (a hot fitness freak), so the idea of him becoming a chocolate bar was odd.

Frank placed a slightly sticky gummy hand on my shoulder and tried to rub it in some strange effort to comfort me. But candy people were still learning what human things they could do. All I felt was Frank rubbing sticky gummy stuff over my shoulder. I didn't pull away, but I wanted to!

Walking away from the crime scene, I waved to Frank.

"Come on Frankie boy, we goanna see someone special,"

***

I had no idea for the past few years my beautiful Michael had been only a few miles from me, I thought he had gone to another country after we split up. If I had known he was so close, I would have kept in touch, watching out for him like he had me all those years ago.

Staring at the massive suburban gingerbread house ahead, I shook my head as I couldn't understand why all Suburbs looked the same. It was strangely unnerving, this gingerbread house was identical to all of the others in the street from the beautiful icing decorations to the chocolate buttons that made up the roof.

A part of me wondered if all the people inside were the same, the same candy, the same attitudes, the same personality, the lot.

Then I thought about my beautiful Michael and how special he was, he wouldn't have been the same, he was honestly the best and kindest person I'd ever met.

Breathing in the honey sweet air of the street, I knew someone here must have kept bees (for something) or turned into some kind of honey candy when they turned. Whatever the reason it smelt great.

Taking a few steps closer to the large gingerbread door ahead of me and Frank, I looked down as I felt the candyfloss path crack and bend under my weight, and even now I was surprised at how the world was after the Awakening.

The sounds of high pitch laughing of hard boiled Candy Children, echoed around the suburb as presumably children played, but I hadn't seen anyone today save me and my team.

As me and Frank walked up to the gingerbread door, it opened and out came a little square chocolate coated biscuit with small icing glasses and eyes.

When I saw Michael's mother I couldn't help but smile, I could see in her small icing eyes that she was just as kind as she was all those years ago.

The little biscuit walked out slowly and her eyes narrowed on me and Frank. (Granted she did seem a little scared of Frank)

"David Alexandria?" she asked, her voice still smooth and wise after all these years.

I nodded.

She smiled at me. "My son's dead isn't he?"

I'm still not sure if candy people could tear up but if I was human I honestly might have cried in that moment. Seeing his mother so sad was bad enough before I considered how I was feeling towards his death.

I nodded.

His mother took a few more steps towards us.

"Michael never stopped talking about you, you know. He loved you after all this time,"

I could only nod again. Not exactly what I wanted to be hearing right now.

"My darling David, you must have questions?"

"Um yea-" I said before I wondered something.

"How did ya know he was… gone?" I asked.

"This is a suburb darling, news travels fast,"

"But I haven't seen anyone here today," I said.

She cocked her head and her icing eyes narrowed on me and Frank.

"You must see the other people. Look behind you," the little biscuit said.

Me and Frank turned around but I didn't see anything. All I saw was the same delicious vanilla ice cream road as earlier with candyfloss making up the pathway. I looked at Frank and he shrugged.

"There's no one here," I said.

The chocolate biscuit cocked its body at us.

"You must see all the hard boiled sweets in the road playing, singing, laughing. What about the chocolate twirls over in the corner?"

I wanted to say something but what could I say? She was clearly seeing people that weren't there. Yet I did feel something behind me.

Trying to ignore the weirdness of the Suburb, I looked at and Frank and I knew he wanted me to ask the questions and get out of here.

"Do you know anyone who could have hurt Michael?"

The little chocolate coated biscuit nodded.

"Of course, it's those people behind you. They all hated Michael because he was a liar like you, he said there weren't any people there,"

I opened my mouth and closed it again, then I saw Frank point towards his head and circle it. I was about to tell him off for calling her crazy but I think she could be, there were no people here.

I felt some of the toffee droplets of sweat freeze on my back. My eyes widened as I wondered if there weren't people here but ghosts.

Didn't ghosts freeze things and make them cold?

"Are you seeing ghosts?" I asked.

The little biscuit stared at us and at the same time wasn't staring at us but behind us. Maybe there were ghosts behind us talking or maybe even gesturing to her.

Slowly Michael's mother nodded to us.

"Can ya ask the ghosts why they killed Michael?" I asked, Frank just looked at me like I was going mad.

"They said he disrespected them. He wanted the ghosts gone. They don't like you either,"

My little toffee heart went faster.

"Why don't they like us?"

"Because you're going to hurt them, arrest them and kill them again,"

"I promise them I not gonna do that," I said, calmly. "Did Michael threaten to do that?"

His mother nodded. "He scared for me. He thought they were going to hurt me,"

"So they hurt him first," I said.

I paused for a few moments as I tried to understand what to do here. I knew Michael's mother wasn't a liar, a madwoman or anything nasty. Even when me and Michael did some things we shouldn't have (at least not at our young age) she wasn't furious, she just sat us down and calmly explained why we shouldn't do it again.

I knew she wasn't lying about the ghosts, I could even feel them but I couldn't arrest ghosts. So there was only one thing I could do.

"Can ya tell the ghosts to promise me never to hurt anyone again? I'll do everything I can to protect 'hem," I said.

Michael's mother smiled and nodded. (Presumably she nodded with the ghosts)

"They promise,"

Me and Frank both smiled so we wished the little chocolate biscuit and the ghosts good day and we left.

***

Driving back to the main city away from this weird little Suburb in our little car made from rhubarb and custard hard boiled sweets, me and Frank sat in silence as I drove. I was pretty sure Frank was asleep but the strange thing about gummy bears was they didn't snore or make much sound so who knows.

As I turned onto the last street with the perfectly identical gingerbread houses, candyfloss pathways and vanilla ice cream roads, I smiled as I was finally going to leave this strange place.

The smell of sweet custard and rich bitter rhubarb filled my nose from the car and as I said earlier, I much preferred my candy life. The smells were a lot better.

The car hummed along as we kept driving but something was bothering me about the whole thing, my beautiful Michael was melted and there were strange little chocolate chunks left in the road. But I couldn't understand how ghosts would be able to do that.

Sure I understood and I truly believed the ghosts were there, I had felt them and Michael's mother wasn't a liar, she must have been some kind of strange medium for the dead. But it still didn't explain how the ghosts were able to kill Michael, my Michael.

Approaching the end of the suburb, I shrugged as I knew I had enough to tell my Captain and close the case, of course my Captain wasn't going to be happy without an arrest.

But you can't arrest ghosts, especially killer ghosts and the world was in a crazy place anyway. I know the story of ghosts being real wasn't going to be laughed at like before the Awakening. So hopefully that truth would keep people happy with me, and keep me my job.

Just as we drove out the suburb and onto the chocolate ice cream road ahead, I looked back in my rhubarb and custard mirror for some reason.

My eyes widened at what I saw, well I thought I saw it, behind me hundreds of ghosts stood on the boundary of the suburb smiling and waving at me. Ghosts of all different candies from caramel to boiled sweets to twirls to ice creams and more.

My eyes narrowed as I saw a large Belgium chocolate bar in the middle waving at me and saying something. It was probably *safe travels* but I don't know.

As I drove off into the distance I took a deep sweet breath and shook my head as I realised how strange of a day it had been. I had lost a great ex-boyfriend, learnt about ghosts and now I have to explain to my Captain how a Belgium chocolate bar ghost killed my ex.

But that challenge excited me, and this was all tomorrow's problem anyway. Today I just wanted to drive back to the city and have a good long drink with Frank and remember the love of my life.

AUTHOR OF BETTIE ENGLISH PRIVATE EYE MYSTERIES
CONNOR
WHITELEY
THE FUTURE
LAW
A MYSTERY SHORT STORY

THE FUTURE LAW

30th September 2040

London, England

Criminal Defence Lawyer Tim Lovejoy sat at his large wonderful wooden desk inside his delightfully large office that was simply perfect for him considering his so-called wobbling, stumbling and gentle banging into things according to his assistant Stephine. Tim naturally didn't believe he did anything of those at all and his little rake-thin assistant was just being so dramatic.

Granted being so dramatic was their delicious bread and butter in the criminal defence world but she just had to be wrong this time.

Even if she was right, Tim enjoyed that his office was easily the size of most flats with only a grey metal filing cabinet, some cheap holo-art that flickered every so often because it was too cheap and his wonderful desk. Most clients instantly believed that it was too bare and Tim was some strange lover of the minimalism design scene.

None of that was true at all.

He just loved having the space to move elegantly about, or apparently stumble and wobble about according to his assistant. But Tim was one day going to prove her wrong and hopefully she should simply put on a bit of weight herself. She was too thin, too damn thin.

The sound of Stephine on the phone outside made Tim roll his eyes. Soon there would be another case to defend and bang his plans for the afternoon would go.

Within minutes too-thin-Stephine would probably bounce happily through the newly painted brown wooden door of the office and tell him of a case, Tim wasn't sure he actually wanted a case today to defend. He had wanted to sneak out for lunch to some sensational fried chicken place two blocks away. He of course wouldn't tell his wife about his lunch because she was obsessed he needed to lose weight, he didn't but she believed it, and Tim wanted to live in peace too much to argue with her.

So the top-secret fried chicken lunches with none of that salad crap would have to be the compromise. A compromise Tim would happily live with.

Tim wasn't too sure but somehow his wife must have gotten Stephine involved in her little scheme because his office smelt so strange, difficult and awful today. There wasn't a single hint of fried chicken, deep fried shrimp or potatoes. The office just smelt so plain of lavender, lilacs and some earthy perfume that Stephine must have sprayed.

Little assistant.

Tim heard Stephine finish up on the phone call outside and he almost got up and "wobbled" over to the silly door but he didn't need to move. Stephine would come to see him and then they could have a great debate about why he needed to defend a case instead of having a sensational fried chicken lunch.

Of course, Tim loved defending cases. He was normally in court five times a day, six days a week because the seventh day of the week was devoted to his wife. He loved defending innocent murderers because the law was so much more sophisticated these days compared to the barbaric 2020s so his job was so amazingly fun.

"Good morning Tim," Stephine said as she came into the office bouncing along like she always did.

"Morning what you got for me today,"

"A great one. A truly great case that will be right up your alley. You get to defend the first man ever accused of the Future Law,"

Tim laughed. He had heard of the Future Law a couple of times in the past week because two months ago the UK Government had bought it in allowing the police to arrest people who were believed to be about to commit a crime in the future. It involved a lot of guesswork and evidence gathering and many in the law community wasn't sure about it at all but it was a fun idea.

Tim had no idea how someone could be prosecuted for a crime they haven't committed yet. But clearly someone was now.

"And as you know all Future Law cases don't go to trial,"

Tim nodded. That was something else that the law community had flat out hated about the new law and because of that little detail lawyers weren't needed in these situations unless the accused (or guilty to be honest) managed to convince a judge that it was needed.

And Tim supposed that because this was the first time the law had been used he didn't exactly imagine that convincing was very hard at all.

"Damn you Sep. I'll grab my coat," Tim said as he got up, grabbed his coat and marched out the door.

And the very idea of being the first ever lawyer to test out the law excited Tim a lot more than he ever wanted to admit.

***

After a quick stop at home to pick up his dataslate because it had access to the most recent legal library of the UK (something his so-called laptop wasn't compatible with these days), Tim arrived in the very dark interrogation room where his client was meant to be meeting him.

The interrogation room wasn't where Tim liked to meet clients but with people accused (or convicted there was no difference in this law) of Future Law crimes not having access to privacy or confidentiality, the interrogation room was the only place where they could meet.

With the cops and judges listening to their every single word.

When Tim had started law in the 2010s he had loved helping clients in secret, talking to them in private and he just knew that it seriously helped him as a lawyer. But he never would have imagined those rules would be gone 30 years later and the impact on his work was becoming clearer and clearer.

It was so much harder to help an innocent person these days.

The interrogation room was basically in pitch black except for the two bright yellow bulbs that shone down over the grey metal table that Tim's client was chained to.

The client was called Mr Bobby Franklin, a very well liked man who taught at a local primary school, he had a husband called Edward and three kids that loved him and he had never committed a crime at all. He donated his money to charity most of the time and he coached a children's football team on weekends.

He was the perfect person.

But apparently the UK Government believed that he was going to murder his best friend and fellow schoolteacher Miss Abagail Johnson. Bobby denied the charges and the evidence was weird.

Tim had never seen these pieces of evidence before, so the prosecution's case relied on the search results of internet history that showed Bobby was researching decomposition, he had bought a shovel and he had bought a bottle of bleach in his weekly shopping.

Tim had no idea how the hell that convinced the government Bobby was a criminal, because Bobby had explained that he was teaching the kids science at school, him and his husband were doing gardening and he had bought the bleach for the family's toilet.

Now Tim had to admit he didn't really know how much weight the bleach argument held considering all toilets were self-cleansing now and most gardens were monitored and styled by artificial intelligence.

Tim had to find out more.

"You're my lawyer then?"

Tim nodded and he really wished there was some case law or something for him to investigate so he had a starting point for this initial meeting. But to be honest this was probably the only meeting he would ever have with this client.

"I'm not guilty or anything you know. I wasn't going to kill my best friend and I would never kill someone,"

Tim smiled and leant forward. "Why did you buy the shovel?"

"Because of the garden I was born before Artificial Intelligence and I helped out my parents in the garden when I was a kid. I wanted to share the experience with my kids,"

That was a good argument but again because there was no damn case law Tim didn't know if that was a legally good argument.

"What about the bleach?"

Bobby laughed. "This is ridiculous. Our self-cleaning function broke and me and my husband cannot afford to take time off to wait for a repair person to come. I bought the bleach so we could have a clean toilet until we can have it repaired,"

It was a good point and Tim had done that a good few times himself because no one liked waiting in for a repair person. It was probably the damn bane of his life waiting around. Yet he had to admit waiting around did mean he often got to eat more fried chicken.

"What's going to happen to me?"

As much as Tim just wanted to lie in that moment he really couldn't. He was a lawyer first and foremost and as much as the new updated Lawyer Code of Ethics emphasised that telling the truth was a thing of the past, Tim still believed in those ideals.

"Unless I can figure out a way to prove you aren't guilty of a crime you haven't committed yet then you will be found guilty, taken to prison and because its murder, you will never see the light of day again,"

"What if I vow never to see Abbie again?"

Tim smiled. That was a hell of an idea and it did sort of cock-up the basic principle of the Future Law perfectly. It would make sure that the future crime never ever happened and it would mean that there was no crime to be found guilty of.

Tim also had no idea if because there was no crime to be found guilty of, if Bobby agreed to not be within 100 metres of Abbie would legally binding still be in effect?

That was an amazing legal question.

Tim really wished he had a cup of coffee or something but he didn't. Little cops and their disrespect towards lawyers.

"That still isn't perfect," Tim said. "The problem is if we set a legal precedence of the government arresting anyone and getting them to sign documents cutting people out of their lives. Think of the abuse that could lead to,"

"Of course. Rich and powerful people could arrest their children's boyfriend and girlfriends to split up couples, they could get friends arrested if they believed they were bad influences and more,"

Tim had to admit Bobby definitely had a clever mind. It was a shame that he was teaching children and not university undergraduates.

"It's impossible to find me innocent isn't it?"

Tim just grinned. The law was so stupid these days and it was just a sign that as much as the UK pretended, paraded and branded itself as a democracy, it seriously wasn't. And it hadn't been since the 2020s.

The law meant nothing, the criminal justice system was a mockery and the entire government stunk of corruption.

"Who did you wrong?" Tim asked.

Bobby smiled. "Do you know as a gay man I used to frequent London clubs and hook up with certain people who would later become politicians?"

Tim nodded. "You hooked up with them, so what? Everyone gay or straight hooks up with people from time to time. I was no different in my youth before I met my wife,"

Bobby laughed. "The problem with clubs for the rich and powerful is that they are filled with hidden cameras. Someone taped me and a certain politician and the footage got released recently,"

"And they blame you,"

"You are a sharp stick,"

Tim pretended to tip his non-existent hat off towards Bobby.

"I am sorry," Tim said standing up because there was nothing he could do anymore but Tim really hoped he could figure out something in the next few hours.

"You tried,"

As the black metal door opened and men with black masks walked in and sieged Bobby, Tim just realised that Bobby would never ever be found innocent because the entire system was rigged these days.

Unless Tim was prepared to set a legal precedence that was just as dangerous to everyone else in the UK than allowing Bobby to disappear away to prison was.

It was save one man and damn everyone else. Or let one man suffer and give possible hope to everyone else.

Tim waved his hands. "I need to draw up a legal contract,"

***

Tim seriously hated himself as he sat back in his massive office and he rested his head on the cold hard wooden surface of his desk and he couldn't believe what he had done. At least he had stormed off earlier and grabbed himself a massive fried chicken lunch large enough for a family of five so he could enjoy something before he damned everyone.

But it was done.

He still couldn't believe the excitement on the judge's face as he excepted the damn contract that meant Bobby could never ever see or be within 200 metres of Abagail again. Or he would be charged with murder without a trial of course.

Tim focused on the rather pretty holo-art and realise his actions weren't bad today. Because this wasn't the 2020s or even 2030s anymore, this was the dawn of a new era of law, when it was nothing more than a mere puppet for its political masters.

And Tim was a mere extension of the puppet that was the law.

Tim smiled as Stephine walked in gesturing that she had another case for him, and even though he had stopped a friendship today to stop Bobby going to prison and he had created a piece of case law that the government was already bouncing on, he was still excited about the future.

Because this was one case, one piece of case law and one single opportunity to test the Future Law legally. There were going to be thousands of other cases, chances and people to help in the future and one day Tim was determined to defeat the Future Law.

It was a stupid idea that a government could judge people based on the idea of them committing a crime that they hadn't yet. It was a law that would be defeated and Tim was going to make sure of that, but was that tomorrow's problem.

As he took the dataslate from Stephine and felt his stomach fill with excitement about the next case, next chance to help someone and next chance to win. Tim had to admit that he utterly loved his job and he knew that the future was going to be very bright indeed.

AUTHOR OF ACCLAIMED AGENTS OF THE EMPEROR SERIES
CONNOR WHITELEY
AGE IS PRISON
A SCIENCE FICTION NEAR FUTURE SHORT STORY

AGE IS PRISON

The thick aroma of death, urine and poo filled the air as I went through the dirty white corridor of the Peace Nursing Home, it was marketed as if it was some heaven for the elderly, a place they would be willing to die in and a place that rivalled all other care homes in the entire country.

I had no idea how long ago those marketing ideas were true, maybe they never were but I didn't really care. I had a job to do and I was going to do it, but I really wished I had bought a gasmask or something. Anything to stop myself having to breathe in the disgusting air of this place.

The corridor I was walking across certainly had potential my mother would say because she was an interior designer before she died sadly. She would probably say the smooth, dirty white walls could be textured or painted anew to create something beautiful.

I might have agreed with her but she was dead now, and she wasn't smelling the place. I had no idea how many decades worth of urine and poo were infused with these walls but I knew the smell was never going.

And that was the detail that made this job so much harder, as my beautiful fit sexy boyfriend Officer Nathan Carter walked behind me (probably staring at my ass) and I cannot lie both of us had great bodies.

Nathan might have been slightly on-duty still as a cop but as plain clothes, he was wearing a very sexy pair of blue jeans, tennis shoes and a nice white shirt. He always looked way better than me in my own black jeans, trainers and white t-shirt.

I was normally a criminal thief, stealing from shops, people and whatever other targets I deemed were too rich before I gave it all to charity (after taking my tiny cut of course) and that was why I was here.

I wasn't only a criminal, I was a rather legendary photographer too. I had taken so many amazing photos (according to the public and my editors) of warzones, nature and people that I had been specially requested by the world's oldest woman alive to take her photo and tell her story.

If it was any other woman then I might have actually denied it, but Michelle Bateman was a legendary artist back in the 2000s and now she was approaching her two hundredth birthday, I was looking forward to picturing her.

As me and wonderful Nathan smiled at a small nurse that popped out of Michelle's room, a loud groaning sound echoed up and down the corridor. I panicked for a moment at the idea Michelle might not be talkative but I realised it was everyone else in this place.

The noises of their groaning, moaning and shouting about creatures going bump in the night disrupted me, and I took a step closer to Nathan. He looked like he wanted to hug me but we were both professional to the core and considering there were so many old folk in here we didn't know how they would react to two men hugging.

And I wasn't going to confirm the "gays are weak" stereotype for love or money so I just kept going towards the nurse.

"She's already for you," she said as she led us into the room.

Considering I had been studying, learning and reading all about Michelle for the past twenty years, I have to admit I thought the room was bigger. But it wasn't. It was just another old person room with a smelly single bed, a small bedside table with perfectly smooth corners and a bin.

The bin was empty and I suppose it was just for decoration more than anything else.

There wasn't a single piece of art, a single personal possession nor any sign that anyone else visited her. I didn't know where she kept her clothes but this room was just sad.

"Michelle," the nurse said smiling. "These nice men are here to see you,"

I just looked at Michelle in awe as she sat there in the cold metal of her prison of her wheelchair. The nurse placed her hands on the back of the wheelchair but Michelle still didn't react.

I didn't know if she didn't care, know we were here or maybe she was off in her own fairy land. No one had photographed her for over five years and no one knew why.

And for some reason after five years of silence, completely deadly silence, she had requested me to come here today.

No one even knew why she was living so long when the average human only lived until a hundred. Some people supposed she was the result of genetic engineering, others proposed she was a freak or witch (I doubt it) and others still propose her family are naturally long-lived.

Whatever the case I was getting creeped out now.

"Are you in there Michelle?" the nurse asked getting more annoyed and concerned about Michelle.

Michelle just sat there staring into space. She didn't rock, she didn't react, she only sat there as a large dribble of spit poured out of her mouth. She was once a famous artist, now she was nothing.

And that almost killed me.

I took out my high-tech camera and knelt down in front of her, the smell of urine was way worse down here than it ever was in the corridor. I wanted this to be a quick job no matter what.

I looked at Michelle would the camera lens and then it happened. She smiled for the briefest of seconds and I just froze.

That would be a legendary photo if I could get the famous artist to smile. Something that no one absolutely no one had managed to achieve before, but I froze.

And as I looked at her through the camera I realised that she wasn't staring into space anymore, she was staring just at me and her eyes showed all the intelligence, heart and emotion that she wanted the world to know.

I had seen the same haunted, horrified look on Michelle's face countless times before. I saw it every time after a hurricane ripped through countries ripping families apart, leaving mothers begging to know what happened to their babies. I saw it in the middle east countless times as soldiers watched their friends die and they longed to join them. And I saw that look in disease-ridden communities where young children had lost their family and were lost in the world now.

Michelle was no different.

All I could do was stare through the lens into the emotional, depressed eyes of a woman who wanted to die so badly.

Her body wasn't some pinnacle of science, it was a prison. She probably couldn't move, speak or do anything but herself away. She was a mind trapped in flesh but she didn't control her flesh, every single day of her life she simply sat there waiting for a day that would never come.

She was never going to die.

And she was always going to sit there just waiting, longing, wanting to die. There was nothing I could do about that but tell her story.

I took the picture of her sharp, intelligent, emotional eyes staring at me, longing for me to kill her.

There was a rumour decades ago that she was a master thief, a killer of abusers and someone who always managed to help others through physical acts as much as her art. If that was true then I knew why she summoned me (I didn't know how she summoned me) but she wanted a fellow thief to see her.

And a fellow thief to save her from even more centuries of pain.

I wasn't a killer though.

"Goodbye Michelle. Thank you for everything," I said walking out.

As I went back towards our small black car, Nathan hugged me and I loved his strong muscular body against mine and I just kissed him gently on the neck as we got into the car.

The seats were soft and Nathan looked like he was about to start driving off, but I popped up the glove compartment where Nathan always kept a back-up pistol. I could save her, I could free Michelle, I could do everything for her that no one had ever offered before.

I could be her saviour.

I picked up the alien cold object in my hand and I hated guns but I wanted to use it for Michelle. Just use it for good this one single time.

"You can't," Nathan said.

I just looked into his beautiful dark brown eyes and I knew he was right, he always was right but maybe he wasn't this time.

"I saw the same look you did and she wants to die babe, but we cannot give it to her. If you kill her then I have to arrest you and then no one will ever see your pictures, read your words or benefit from your *borrowing* ever again. How many people would suffer then?"

I nodded and so badly wanted to kiss him but he simply took the gun out of my hand, put it away and he squeezed my leg in love.

"The best thing you can do for her is tell her true story and stress that she wants to die. Someone will figure it out," Nathan said.

I kissed him and as we drove away I realised that was exactly what I was going to do. I was going to write the best article I could, show the world her picture and explain that this was a woman that wanted, longed for and needed to die.

But I died fifty years later and no one helped Michelle.

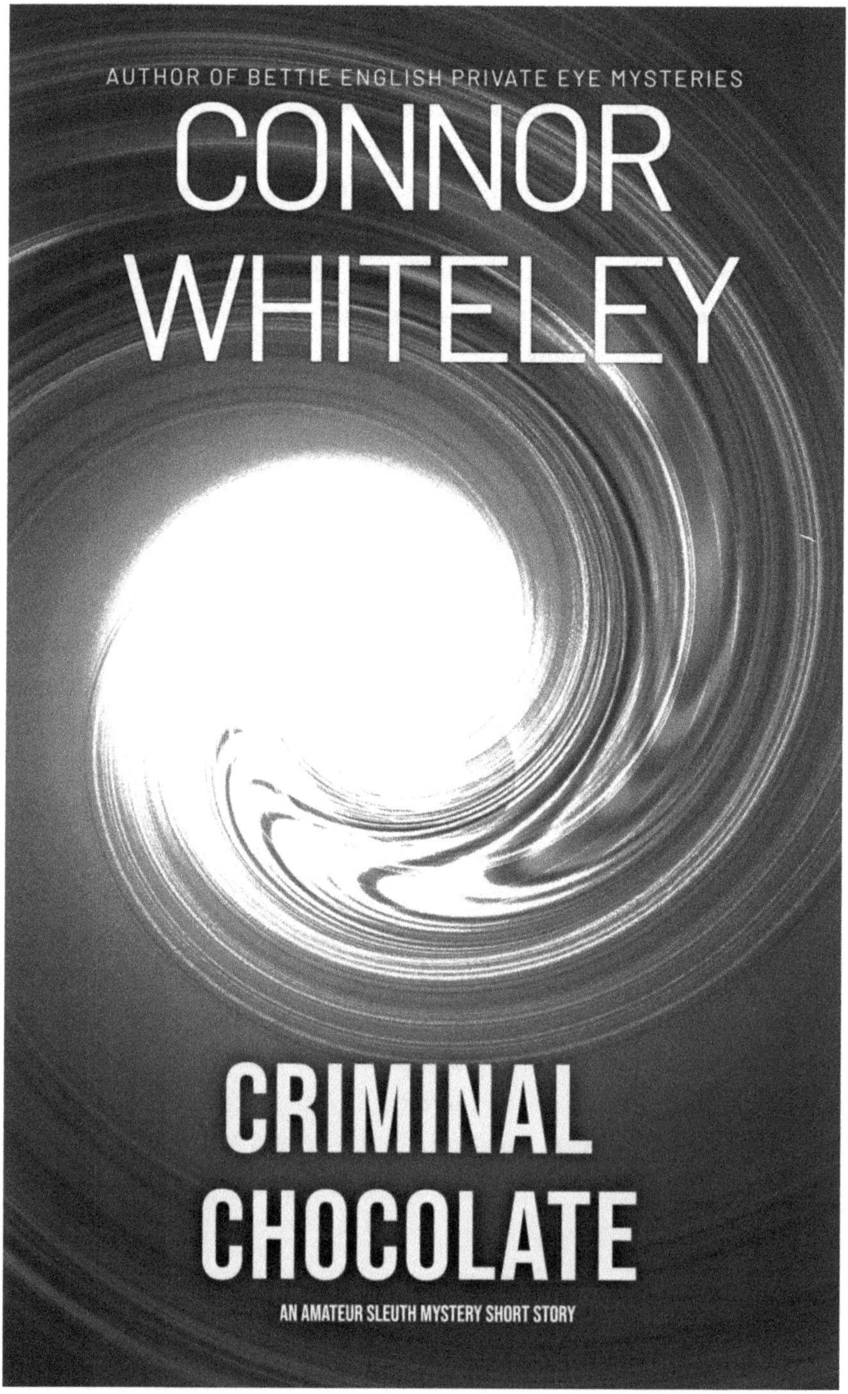
AUTHOR OF BETTIE ENGLISH PRIVATE EYE MYSTERIES
CONNOR
WHITELEY
CRIMINAL
CHOCOLATE
AN AMATEUR SLEUTH MYSTERY SHORT STORY

CRIMINAL CHOCOLATE

The chocolate must have come alive!

Don't get me wrong, I know that is just crazy. It sounds rubbish and like I should be drugged up and locked away so my so-called craziness couldn't hurt anyone.

But it must be the truth!

At least that's what I thought as I stared at the smashed up chocolate bar on the cold wooden floor of my ex-husband's chocolate shop. He was a great guy but I didn't want some cheap chocolate shop in the divorce, and now I'm looking at a smashed up chocolate bar. I'm starting to think I might be right about that.

The smell of sweet rich chocolate filled the air and I loved that smell, it was one of the few benefits of having a chocolate shop, but all that smell was coming from the dead chocolate at my feet. Its sticky caramel "Blood" was everywhere.

The massive caramel stripes that looked like blood spatter decorated the entire floor. It was everywhere! And I was fuming, absolutely fuming that I now had to spend a good hour cleaning the floor, polishing it and preparing it for my customers.

But I couldn't shake the feeling that something was off. The "blood" spray looked too similar to the spray I saw last night on a murder programme. It was exactly like someone small had smashed him (or her) to death, and the caramel "blood" had splashed everywhere as a result.

My crazy silence was broken when I looked up and saw a little boy with his mum and dad tapping the glass and pointing to all the chocolate I had in the front window displays. I couldn't blame him. I had sweet juicy cakes, crunchy biscuits and even my personal favourite, chocolate eclairs that looked like pieces of art. It had amazed me and all my past boyfriends how I hadn't put on any weight after running this place (truth be told, I do have a few secret gyms sessions a week).

When the mum and dad started to drag their son away, I looked back at the smashed up chocolate bar and out of the corner of my eye, I could have sworn I saw something moving. I looked and only saw three fallen over chocolate bars.

That was weird.

I was never careless. I always made sure every single piece of chocolate, biscuit and cake looked perfect in the store. It was what my customers deserved, if they were going to pay and part with their hard earned cash. Then I needed to do my part.

Those chocolate bars should never have fallen over.

But here I was, feeling their freezing cold wrapping as I placed them back where they were meant to be. And it was also rather strange how I could have sworn they were standing up a moment ago.

Maybe I really was going crazy. Maybe I needed more sleep. Maybe I just needed to take a few days off. That might be a good idea, I know my second-in-command Susie could run the shop perfectly for a week or two. I could always go to the Caribbean, Canada or Crete like me and my ex always wanted but he was always "too busy".

I stretched my neck and ran my fingers along all the chocolate shelves that covered every square inch of the walls. I wanted people to walk into the chocolate shop and be stunned at the sheer number of shapes, sizes and types of chocolate that we offered.

And I always got that effect.

After double checking no more chocolate had been knocked over by accident (or magic), I went to go into the back room and grab my cleaning equipment when I heard some muttering coming from my left.

I turned and my eyes narrowed. It was crazy but it sounded as if the chocolate bars were talking to themselves. I took a step closer and they went silent.

As soon as I started to go to the backroom, pick up my supplies and start cleaning, the chocolate bars were muttering to themselves. It was crazy, right? Chocolate bars couldn't talk to each other.

The logical thing to ask or at least consider would be the neighbouring stores each side of me were being loud. But that was impossible since both stores next to me were empty, I suppose some of the homeless kids that I gave the going-out-of-date items to might have been there.

Yet since the police sadly arrested a bunch of them for no good reason, I hadn't seen them for a while. It couldn't be them. Leading me back to my crazy idea in the first place, the chocolate bars had to be talking.

Trying to forget about that craziness, I simply scooped up the smashed up chocolate bar, binned it and started washing the floor.

"That wasn't very respectful," a tiny voice said to me.

That was it! I was going crazy. I had to be going mad, this wasn't normal, surely?

"Ha! Come on John look how scared she is," another voice said to me.

"Who's there?" I asked.

Then three massive chocolate bars (they were cheap chocolate by the way) with their bright red, purple and white packing hopped off the top shelf and landed on the ground.

They all looked identical to me but by the way they were "looking" at each other made me think maybe they could see the subtle differences of each other.

"What are you?" I asked.

"Typical Pinkie Thing. She don't even respect us. She just sells us," the one on the end said in a deep voice.

"Pinkie Thing?" I asked.

"Calm down John. She doesn't know us because Pinkie Things don't know us," the middle one said.

At least I knew they had names, but it still didn't help me understand what they were. They could have been aliens, magic or simply a hallucination?

"Pinkie Thing?" I asked.

John hopped up and down. "Yes! You are a Pinkie Thing. Great Rings of Saturn, don't you creatures know what you are? Or are you too dim for that?"

Oh yes, these were definitely aliens. Damn, I was actually hoping for magic.

"We don't call ourselves Pinkie Things. I am a human. What are you?" I said firmly.

All three chocolate bars hopped over to each other to form a tight little circle and they started muttering. I was surprised they were muttering perfect English but for some reason I really doubted they knew that.

They hopped out into a perfectly straight line again.

"Human?" they all asked.

I nodded.

"Um," the middle one said. "You're not a Pinkie Thing?"

I opened my mouth but closed it and just shook my head.

They all hopped to each other onto a circle again.

Now this was a bit strange because they honestly sounded so confused and shocked. If these were aliens then, for starters, they couldn't be very good ones and most importantly they clearly didn't know what Pinkie Things actually were.

In a strange way I suppose I could understand the confusion because humans are pink on the inside and sometimes on the outside, but clearly these aliens knew humans and Pinkie Things weren't the same.

They popped out into a straight line again.

"Do *you* know what a Pinkie Thing is?" the middle one asked.

I decided maybe it was just best to help these aliens, at least then they could leave and I could finish clearing up my shop. But I had to remember to ask them about this "murdered" chocolate bar.

"There are lots of pink things on this planet. Can you give me details?"

They quickly hopped together, muttered a bit more and went back to their perfectly straight line.

"Of course, Pinkie Things are massive pink things that humans like to eat. They have a strange nose you call a… oh yes a snout and you people say they go… what was it… oink, oink,"

Strangely enough there was actually something rather adorable about three little chocolate bars trying to make pig noises. Yet that made the question of why did they want pigs come to mind. It was going to be a weird answer I know that for sure.

"I think you want pigs. But why?" I asked.

"Of course, I told ya they were called that!" John shouted.

The other two bars just hopped in a way that made me think they were shrugging and wanting to move on.

"Thank you. Sorry to bother you. We must go and find some pigs now," the middle one said.

I waved my hands. "Wait a minute. I'll take you to some pigs if you tell me what that chocolate murder was on my floor and what are you?"

As the middle bar hopped towards me, the other two started to hop towards the door.

"We have… you would call Spies. We infiltrate planets, take the form of something and spy on our prey. We thought this was a Pinkie Thing shop. We apologise for any concern caused,"

Well at least they were polite.

"Why do you need pigs? Why did you kill that chocolate bar?" I asked.

"Wow! Humans do ask a lot of questions. It's simple really, that chocolate was an enemy spy that infiltrated our infiltration. He wanted a pig first for his Masters then we had to kill him before he killed us. I'm really sorry for the mess,"

I could sort of understand that, if TV's taught me anything then it's spies are weird, crazy and never try to understand them fully.

"It's okay. The pigs?"

"Of course human, beyond your little planet is a vast empire and we intercepted one of your transmissions once from your space station to this planet. You were talking about superweapon coded name Bacon, our top intelligence people set to work immediately for your superweapon and for your superweapon to work, it needs a pig,"

Wow!

I actually had no idea what to say. These aliens actually thought Bacon was a code name for a superweapon. Wow! If I had ever ever ever believed Earth was in danger from alien invasion, I think it's fair to say we're safe now.

But there's no reason the aliens need to know that, is there?

***

A few minutes later, I leant against the warm metal fence a pig pen with the horrific smell of mud, pigs and pig poo assaulting my senses and the horrible sounds of pigs talking filled my ears.

It wasn't the best of places but as I watched the three little chocolates jump onto the pig and teleport it away, I actually felt strange and a little… unnerved in a way. Those aliens had no idea what they were doing, at least there was no one else around.

I don't think I could have dealt with anyone asking me about hopping chocolate bars and disappearing pigs. I was really glad I was the only one at the pig pens at this time in the morning.

As I started to make my way through the little muddy footpaths back towards the high street and my shop, I couldn't help myself but wonder about the aliens and what they would do now. They had a pig and surely their top intelligence people had learnt enough about bacon to know how to mass produce it.

So I suppose after all of this, the aliens wouldn't learn about Earth's so-called superweapon but at least they might discover an amazing treat. I did love bacon and maybe to remember all of this craziness, I might create a chocolate bar with tiny pieces of crispy salty bacon.

I never would have liked the idea before, but after my "first contact" maybe I did like the idea. Maybe I needed to see me getting the chocolate shop as a blessing rather than a curse.

As I went onto the high street, I couldn't believe how excited I was for the rest of the day and the rest of my life. I loved my chocolate shop and maybe those criminal chocolate bars (they did kill someone after all) had given me the best gift of all.

They had given me a newfound love for humans, aliens and most importantly chocolate.

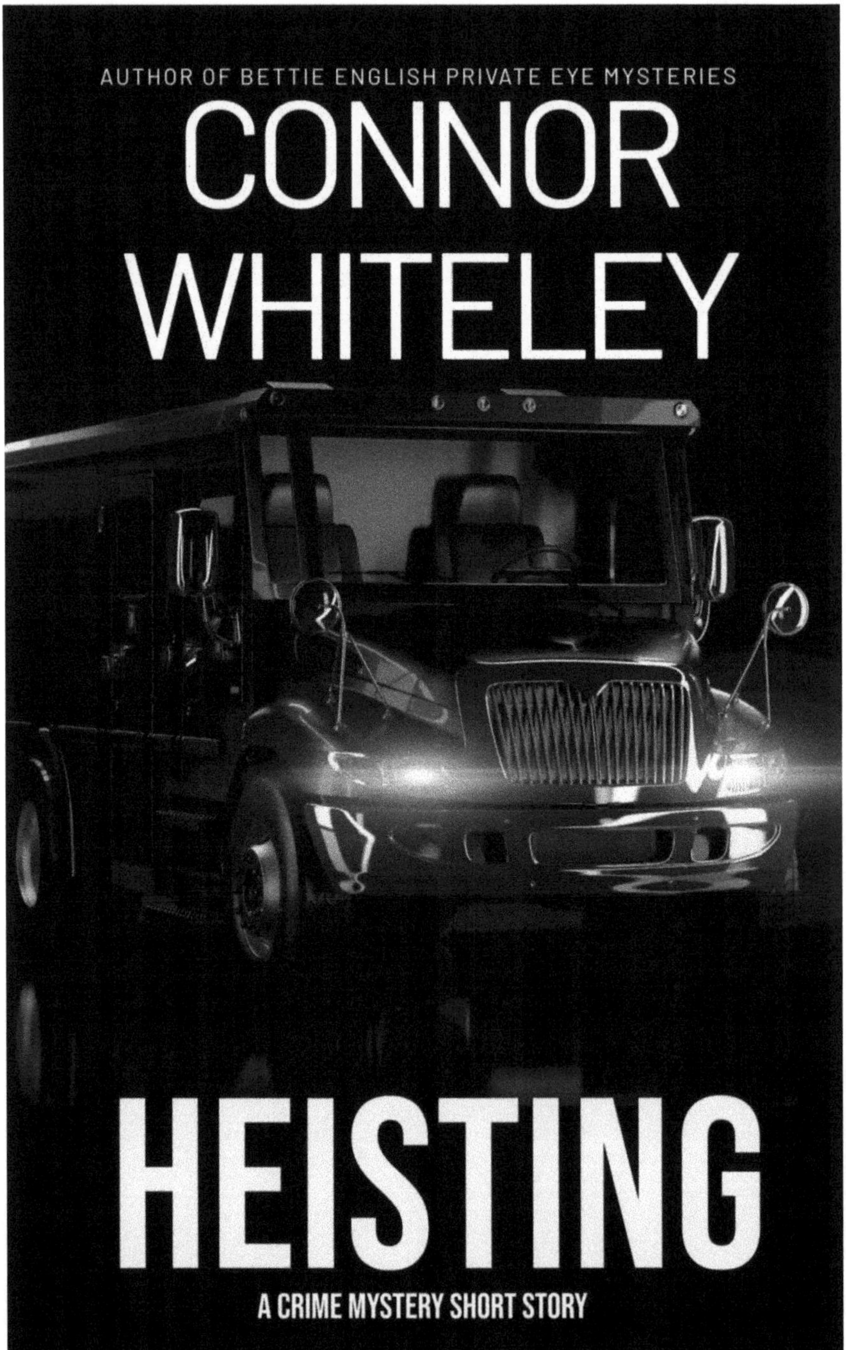
AUTHOR OF BETTIE ENGLISH PRIVATE EYE MYSTERIES
CONNOR
WHITELEY
HEISTING
A CRIME MYSTERY SHORT STORY

HEISTING

Of all the small, tiny cafes filled with strong tobacco smoke, garlic bread and bitter coffee Mae Evans had ever visited or been summoned to. The "Dog's Breakfast" had to be one of the most interesting she had ever been in.

She sat at a tiny brown wooden table that she didn't dare touch because of the strange rough texture that made her fingers sticky with something she seriously didn't want to think about. It could have been alcohol, sweat or spit from the night before but Mae seriously didn't want to touch the table. Especially in case the sticky substance was a lot worse than spit.

Mae was just annoyed that the metal chair wasn't much better. It was perfectly warm considering the awful coldness outside, but she hated the sharp metal screw sticking in her back. She had tried to move a few times but it was useless, the screw wasn't moving and it was going to keep digging in her back until she had met with her friends.

The loud ring of the bell above the wooden door echoed around the entire café, and Mae didn't dare look straight up in case that drew attention to her. If it was one of her friends then they would find her, it was simply the way things worked as a thief and a small group of con people.

Mae subtly looked around at the other tiny tables. The café was rather empty but with the state of the sticky table that shouldn't have been that much of a surprise. She definitely wasn't coming back and she was tempted to give their leader, Awen, an earful about this awful place.

There were a few older men in long black trench coats covered in cigar burn holes sitting about. They were smiling, laughing and smoking their life away and Mae was so glad she had left that life behind. Now she was free to con people, go to school and help innocent people like she had always wanted to.

"Morning darling," Andrew said wearing his normal jeans, white shirt and black shoes as he pulled out a sticky chair next to her and sat down.

Mae wasn't sure if she was thrilled or not to see Andrew of all people arrive here first. She wasn't that fussed by him but he was a good computer person and he was kind enough, even if he did keep staring at her breasts when he thought she wasn't looking.

She hated that about him.

"Sorry I'm late peeps," Awen said as she joined them in her typical long sweeping white dress.

Mae didn't have a clue why Awen would wear such a thing to this café of all places. As soon as Awen went to leave the dress would be black, Mae just shook her head. She was glad she was wearing her typical black tracksuit and her blond bowl-cut so she looked like a boy to most people.

"We have a problem my most wonderful friends," Awen said grinning.

"Why are you so happy for a change?" Mae asked knowing there was a job coming. "It certainly isn't because of the coffee or food this place serves,"

"Oh I don't know darling, I mean it seems friendly enough here," Andrew said.

Mae waved him silent and looked at Awen.

"We have a very exciting job today," Awen said. "You remember a few weeks ago I said my grand-uncle Scott had thankfully been murdered by my father,"

"Yes," Mae said smiling. She had no idea how someone could be so damn happy about a murder.

“Are you sure that’s a good thing darling?” Andrew said knowing he wouldn’t be happy with a murder. “I mean he was your family and you did love him a lot,”

“I mean Scott was a wonderful man,” Awen said sort of understanding why they thought she didn’t love him, “but Scott’s death means we have a lot of opportunity,”

“Why?” Mae asked.

“The problem with my father being the killer is that it means several shipments of highly valuable gold and Laser weaponry have to be moved from his factories,”

Mae nodded. She had always loved stories from Awen about her and her family being rich and having a ton of government contracts that meant the family got to protect the UK’s gold supplies, and transport any individual components of the UK’s new laser weaponry programme.

Clearly those contracts had now been revoked, for good reason.

“In a few hours,” Awen said, “the UK government is moving some of the gold in massive hover truck that is going to drive through our path. It isn’t armed, it isn’t escorted and it isn’t hard to steal from,”

Mae shook her head. “This doesn’t make sense. We know that the government always escorts gold because it is the only thing supporting the UK economy. If the UK loses its gold then the pound devalues even more,”

“It already costs me a hundred pounds for a loaf of bread darling,”

Mae caught Andrew staring at her breasts and it took her everything she had not to slap him.

“So what’s the plan then?” Mae asked.

Awen leant forward. “I am the leader and charmer, Andrew is the computer person and you are the thief. This all comes down to you and your skills after Andrew has hacked into the truck and I have charmed the driver into submission,”

Mae smiled because she loved jobs like this. There wasn't a good plan, there wasn't a chance of escape and there was a lot of gold at stake. She could help a hell of a lot of people with all that wonderful gold.

"Let's get planning," Mae said.

***

A few hours later, Mae leant on the icy cold wooden wall of a bright red shop as she watched an endless stream of people in all their different dresses, suits and casual clothes go up and down the cobblestone high street. She had no idea why a group of young women were wearing short skirts in this weather, it wasn't normal and it certainly wasn't right.

It was probably why she liked her tracksuit so much. It was comfortable, warm and because she didn't look like a girl no one really noticed her, exactly how she wanted it.

She wasn't a fan of how all the little and large market stalls and shops in their varying shades of blues, reds and greens made the high street seem ancient and unloved. There was a lot of paint falling off the side and window trims.

But she supposed that just reminded her a lot about the UK at the moment, there was no money for anyone and each day thousands, if not tens of thousands, were getting poorer and were struggling to put food on the table. Yet it was also those people that gave her the strength to keep going and committing these cons.

A loud bang in the distance and a minor surge in heat made Mae smile as she watched a massive grey ugly hover truck zoom forward in the distance.

The truck wasn't much to look at but it was reinforced, heavy as steel and Mae knew there was no way to break into it. It was impossible to force your way into a hover truck unless you knew exactly what you were doing.

Mae looked across the high street and saw Awen in her sweeping white dress and Andrew was probably somewhere too staring at her breasts. Mae really wanted to teach him a lesson but now wasn't the time.

The hover truck banged and hummed and vibrated a few times and Awen went over to it. Mae made sure to hang back for now so she slowly went through the crowd and watched as Awen did her thing. Awen went straight over to the two male drivers as the hover truck smashed onto the ground.

She tried to be helpful and Mae read her lips so she knew Awen was talking about being a mechanic and being able to help them.

Mae had no idea if that was true but Awen was extremely clever, confident and she was sure Awen could sell thousands of mice to an elephant if the situation called for it. She really was that good.

Mae pulled up her black hoody on her tracksuit and went through the crowd now the drivers were distracted.

A lot of people had gathered to see what was happening but Mae didn't doubt they would be silent *if* they saw her.

She went over to the immense back of the truck where there were no door handles, only a seam where the back split open and a small electronic keypad.

Mae typed in the standard government codes and none of them worked. It shouldn't have been that hard considering all the hover trucks used the exact same security system. It was almost annoying she didn't have Andrew in her ear so she could talk to him, but she had already done that once. She had hated his heavy seductive breathing in her ear even more.

And he actually did it without realising.

Mae tried typing in various standard passwords that Awen had mentioned her father's company used.

Nothing worked.

Mae went towards the driver's compartment and listened to what Awen was saying to them. Mae just knew when Awen realised there was a problem she would be able to do anything.

Mae really wanted to get inside in the driver's compartment so she could manually open the back of it. Then she could grab the bags of gold without anyone knowing.

"You idiot!" Awen shouted.

Mae smiled as everyone was moving around so they could see Awen and the two drivers, who were now getting out of the driver's compartment.

"You two are the biggest idiots I have ever seen. No wonder the hover truck crashed when you two don't even know how it works," Awen shouted. "Do you not realise these machines need to be cared for?"

"Go away lady. We'll simply call for support. We don't need you or your skills or your attitude,"

"Really! Attitude! Oh you have no fucking idea about my attitude towards idiots yet matey," Awen said.

Mae laughed, Awen was seriously good at her job and she was providing a perfect distraction.

Mae gripped the grey door handle, pulled it open and silently slipped inside. The standard design of the driving compartment with only two small black chairs and a wide range of buttons and switches was a bit of a letdown but she had to focus.

She kept her head down and focused on the massive buttons, one of them had to be the controls for the back door.

"I am calling the police unless you go away," a driver said.

Mae found the big button that was labelled "Door Controls". She pressed it and heard the minor hiss of the hydraulic valves opening the back doors.

She slipped out of the truck and almost smiled as the icy coldness of the cobblestones made her feel alert and focused as she went to the back of the hover truck.

Mae pulled open the back door of the hover truck but it was empty. There was no gold, no laser weaponry, no nothing in the back of the truck.

It was completely empty.

Mae went round to look at the two drivers and Awen looked surprised to see her, so Mae pulled down her black hoody and simply stared at the two drivers.

"The gold is empty. Where is it?" Mae asked.

"Thief!" a driver shouted. "I'll call the police,"

Awen stepped forward. "And what? Explain what you did with all the gold that was behind there. Are you seriously going to keep the gold for yourselves when so many innocent people need it?"

Mae smiled as Awen started to use "The Tone". She knew the drivers wouldn't last a minute under Awen's sweet ritual.

"Look around you," Awen said. "Look these brave men and women around you are hungry, uncertain about their future and they want to know if they'll be able to put food on the table. You have the power to make a choice,"

Mae nodded to reinforce the point.

"You have the power to change lives today and you have the power to give innocent families hope for a better tomorrow. Do you want that?"

Mae watched the two drivers but she could see the fear in their eyes and she realised this wasn't about *them* per se. This was about something far, far greater and she wouldn't have been surprised if these two people had already "gifted" the gold to a criminal or something.

"Who did you give it too?" Mae asked.

"He will kill us," a driver said.

Mae laughed. "Look around you. I think this crowd might kill you,"

Mae hated saying the words but she could see the rage, the outrage and the sheer tension in the faces of everyone watching this. The young and old, fat and slim and male and female all wanted a piece of these men.

Because everyone knew the economy and the value of the pound depended on gold these days, the less gold the UK had the more extreme the prices were.

"Douglas Harrison," a driver said.

Mae nodded her thanks and simply left with Awen up the high street and they both left the crowd to do whatever they wanted with the two drivers that had almost cost them even more than the current economic climate had already.

But Mae knew Douglas Harrison, a major international criminal mastermind, was a little beyond their reach so as much as Mae didn't want to do it, she was going to have to call in the police.

And just hope beyond hope the police gave them what they wanted and stealing from the police was always easy.

***

Mae was rather surprised a few days later as she was driving a huge black police evidence van in her black tracksuit, that the police had actually done their job the first time and to the letter. They had raided Douglas Harrison's home, they had arrested him and they had managed to recover far more gold than they ever thought possible.

Mae really enjoyed the sweet hints of coffee, doughnuts and chocolate ice cream that filled the evidence van, and made the great taste of summer picnics with her family form on her tongue. Awen was sitting next to her and Andrew was sitting in the back with all the gold, that way he couldn't stare at her breasts anymore.

Mae went felt damn happy with herself as she applied the handbrake at a red light, for being a part of this con and the police honestly believed they were real evidence handlers and they were heading to the police station to log in all the gold. Of course the gold wasn't going to reach the police lockup, it was all going to go to the amazing, innocent people that needed it most.

She couldn't wait to see their happy little faces and she would certainly sleep easier knowing that for thousands of families, life had just gotten a little easier. And that was an amazing thing to do.

As the light turned green Mae started to slowly speed off again into the sunset, she was so happy to have Awen and even Andrew by her side because they achieved great things together, they were great friends and most importantly heisting made a positive difference to a lot of lives.

And that was an amazing thing to realise driving off into the sunset.

AUTHOR OF BETTIE ENGLISH PRIVATE EYE MYSTERIES
CONNOR WHITELEY
PRIDEFUL KILLING
AN ASSASSIN CRIME FICTION SHORT STORY

PRIDEFUL KILLING

I, hitman Darren Ward, have to admit that right now as I leant against the warm red brick wall of a local pub set in a beautiful Tudor-style house in southeast England, I really would rather be anywhere else. I would rather like to be reading to the elderly, cleaning up after the elderly at the local old people's home and I would much rather be singing softly to the sick children at the local children's hospital.

But instead I am leaning against the red bricks of a pub just waiting for my target to walk out of there. The pub itself was actually in a very nice area that I really liked, all across the high street were sweet little Victorian shops painted in reds, blues and dark greens.

All the shops were starting to flake at the edges, some shops had their single-glazed windows smashed and boarded up but it was the roses, tulips and sweet marigots that made me smile. It was even better that the warm evening sunshine was lighting up the sky with immense streaks of fiery orange as the sun started to set.

There were plenty of cute happy cutes walking about holding hands, they were some kissing and others laughing. The young women were beautiful in long sweeping summer dresses and the men were even more stunning in their tight-fitting jeans, fit shirts and beautiful piercing eyes.

Maybe only a handful of men had piercing eyes but I was glad that everyone else was having a great night out, because I wasn't.

I seriously wasn't having a good night.

I understand that there are homophobes in the world, I have suffered through more homophobia than I care to admit and I had seen the destructive power of that hatred in more ways than one ever since I was a child. Yet when my boyfriend, a local science teacher at a local secondary school, gets attacked, beaten up and ends up in hospital fighting for his life just because he loves men.

That is when I disobey The Firm and I kill people I am not sanctioned to kill.

Normally I kill serial killers, I kill drug lords and I kill terrorists. I actually hate killings but considering I donate 50% of my earnings to charity and I am a millionaire by nature, I actually don't mind it.

And it gets evil people off the street.

That was why I was happily waiting outside this pub on Rochester high street just waiting for my target to come out, because I was going to kill him.

I have to admit it wasn't exactly hard for me to track him down because that's the thing about homophobes, they are actually rather dumb and they always have a tiny little prick of a penis too.

True story that.

So after my boyfriend had been rushed into the operating theatre and the doctors assured me that they were trying but he probably was going to die, I set to work and I am still waiting for the nurses to call me saying he was out of the theatre.

As soon as I had kissed my wonderful boyfriend on the head, I had gotten into my small black car and I had hacked into the security cameras surrounding the school. I had watched the attack first hand.

I had no idea why Little Prick had felt the need to take a crowbar to my boyfriend's head, junk and body but he was going to die for it. Little Prick hadn't even had the brain cells to cover his face so I simply ran facial recognition through my mobile phone.

There really was an app for everything these days.

And I had found a match, Little Prick was called Tyler Page, a rather attractive 25-year-old man from Strood, he had never finished secondary school, he wasn't employed and judging by his mock scores on his GSCEs, he was as dumb as a bag of rocks.

Exactly like all homophobes as far as I was concerned.

"I hate Pride Month," a man said.

I subtly looked over towards the entrance to the pub and shook my head as I realised the very tall, ugly, elderly man wasn't my target. He was just another drunk, drinking homophobe who was going to go and spread hate and rage all around the local area.

He was even carrying leaflets about why God was right and gays were fundamentally diseased.

Thankfully I am a very effective hitman so I simply flicked my wrist and a very tiny bullet flew through the air out of my high-tech wrist gun.

The bullet splashed against his head and I just watched as the contact-poison started to work its way into his bloodstream.

He would be dead in two hours. The poison would be completely untraceable and a post-mortem would simply reveal heart attack.

No I am not sorry.

I felt the cold metal barrel of a gun against the back of my head.

"Gay," a man said.

I smiled as I slowly turned around and I saw Little Prick standing just there just grinning at him. Normally I don't grin at my prey but I actually did today because I knew the homophobe was going to die.

I wasn't going to lie. Tyler Page was not a *bad*-looking man at all, his deep emerald eyes were very average, his body was fit and skinny but it looked like I was right to call him Little Prick.

"Get in the back alley," Tyler said to me.

I simply shook my head as I noticed other people were starting to notice the gun being pointed at me.

I knew from basic psychology that the Bystander Effect would mean that no one called the cops because everyone thought that someone else would simply do it. I don't blame them but it hardly made me feel any safer.

Thankfully I was a very good assassin.

I went round the other side of the pub and down a very narrow cobblestone alley that was shrouded in darkness. There weren't any lights, any puddles or any signs of life in the alley.

It was just me and my target and all my assassin tricks up my sleeve.

You might be asking why I didn't simply kill him there and then, I seriously could and I could make sure the body was never found so The Firm was okay, but I wasn't a monster like Tyler.

I wanted to give him a choice. Repent or death.

I smiled at Tyler. "Why did you attack my boyfriend?"

Tyler laughed. "Come on man, your species is disgusting and he was a school teacher for crying out loud,"

I couldn't help but smile because he was being silly.

"What you smiling at fag?" he asked.

"What are you scared of?" I asked looking around in case there was something in my environment I could use to help me.

There wasn't.

"I am not scared man. I ain't no pussy like you and your *boy*friend. I am a man. I just wanna protect the kids but peos like you,"

I frowned. He was one of *those* homophobes.

"What risk would I ever pose to a child for God sake?" I asked really wanting to do nothing more than snap his body in half.

"Everyone knows that gays hurt kids and groom them. Gays always groom children, man, that is how your kind work and a schoolteacher is the perfect position for a predator,"

I whacked the gun out of his hand.

I grabbed the gun with my other hand and activated a small superheated blaster in my hand that melted the gun and I threw it on the ground.

I loved the toys The Firm gave me.

"A School teacher, man," Tyler continued. "I heard from my little sister that your *boy*friend was teaching gay content to kids. My little 15-year-old sister was learning about gays. That is wrong man,"

I shook my head because I knew exactly what my boyfriend was teaching those kids and it wasn't dangerous at all.

"How is teaching kids the history of gay rights a bad thing? How is teaching children that gay and straight people are no different a bad thing? How is teaching that you will meet a gay person and they aren't a danger to you, a bad thing?"

"But they are a danger man," Tyler said. "What about the news?"

"What about it? The news will always pick up on the most sensational, most scary, most outrageous pieces of information because it makes you watch it. If a straight person attacks someone on the same day as a gay person does the exact same thing what will be reported,"

"The straight attack because everything is set against straight people," Tyler said.

I tried to smile at him because I could see that he wasn't a bad person, he was just misinformed and I didn't want to kill him.

I really didn't.

"No," I said. "I am sorry about whatever you went through to make you think straight people are disadvantaged but I promise you that isn't true,"

Tyler frowned at me.

He charged.

He kicked.

He whipped out a knife.

I didn't think. Only reacted.

I stepped to one side.

Tyler flew past me.

I grabbed his wrist with the knife.

I snapped it.

He didn't stop.

He punched me.

He went to get me in a headlock.

I got him in a headlock first. "Please stop this Tyler,"

"You fags can't even defeat me. A bright strong white man. We will stop you. We will stoop you grooming children. We will-"

I snapped his neck before he could finish another word. I had given him a chance or two or three so he could hopefully change his mind but he wouldn't.

I have had to deal with people like him my entire life, from my own parents who kicked me out at aged 14 when The Firm found me, to my first kill three years later and to my brothers and sisters when I found them three years after that.

Everyone has hated me in the past but I actually don't worry because I am a survivor and I know not everyone hates gays. In fact a lot of people don't actually care if you're gay or not.

It is simply the haters that care and that's a good thing.

My phone rang and I simply hoped that was good news from the operating theatre.

***

After dying twice in surgery, losing more litres of blood than I care to think about and one of the doctors having a heart attack during the op, I was thankfully sitting in a small wooden chair next to the sterile white hospital bed of my boyfriend.

The hospital room was way too cold and sterile and clinical for me, and I was an assassin so I was used to that sort of stuff. Its white walls were odd, the old blue vase on a wooden bedside table next to me was the only colour in the room and the nurses were thankfully leaving me alone.

I had managed to find a very empty bin at the bottom of the alleyway, I was fairly sure that was where Tyler had wanted to put my body, and I was happy to exchange his body for mine. Of course I had placed some nanobots in there too so his body would be dissolved into a hard lump of fat in an hour and no one would ever know that Tyler was dead.

I guess I have to thank Tyler for choosing an alley with no cameras on either side of it.

I stared at the beautiful man I loved as he gently stirred. I hated it how his arms and legs were covered in metal rods, plaster and more medical equipment than I knew the names of. His face was still as soft, handsome and stunning as the day we had first met at university.

He had a bursted lip, cuts covered his face and he had two black eyes but he was alive and that was all that mattered.

I presume he went to look at me but he couldn't because of the brace around his neck so I stood up and went over to him. He weakly smiled as soon as he saw me.

"He's gone," I said simply.

I could have sworn that he frowned but I didn't care. He was a teacher and I was an assassin, we both helped to make the world a better place in our own little hands. Mine were just a little less legal than his.

"Why?" he asked weakly and I hated listening to how much pain he was in.

"Because he believed in the myths, the lies and the extreme misconceptions about gay teachers," I said.

There was no point lying to him because I loved him, I had no reason to lie to him, just like how straight people had no reason to lie to their partner about their job.

"Maybe I shouldn't have taught that single lesson. It was the only one I was going to do on it anyway," he said.

I laughed and went to hold his hand but I knew exactly how much pain he was in so I didn't. I really wanted to though.

"My beautiful man, my silly beautiful man. You did nothing wrong here and you know how important teaching children about discrimination, racism and hate is,"

"Sometimes it only seems to breed more hate,"

I shook my head. "No, children need to be exposed to new ideas, new concepts and new hopes if you suffer at home. School is about realising there is more to life than what parents talk about, and children need to know that gay, black people and everyone else are okay,"

My boyfriend tried to smile but I could tell it pained him too much.

"School is about teaching children that everything will be okay. It doesn't matter if you're straight, gay, black, white, whatever. If we all realise that being different isn't dangerous then we will help to make the world a better place. That is the point of having one or two or maybe even more lessons during Black History Month, Pride Month and everywhere else in the year,"

"We give kids that are different hope," he said.

I smiled. I really did love him and he really was the most amazing man that I had ever met.

So I got out my holo-phone, opened a new romance book I just bought earlier in the day and I started reading.

I normally read for the elderly and I always would, but until my beautiful boyfriend was healed again. I was going to read to him and tell him wonderful stories of love, happiness and joy where everyone was equal and hate was a thing of the past.

We can all dream of a better future and I was proud to be a part of it by pridefully killing hate one person at a time.

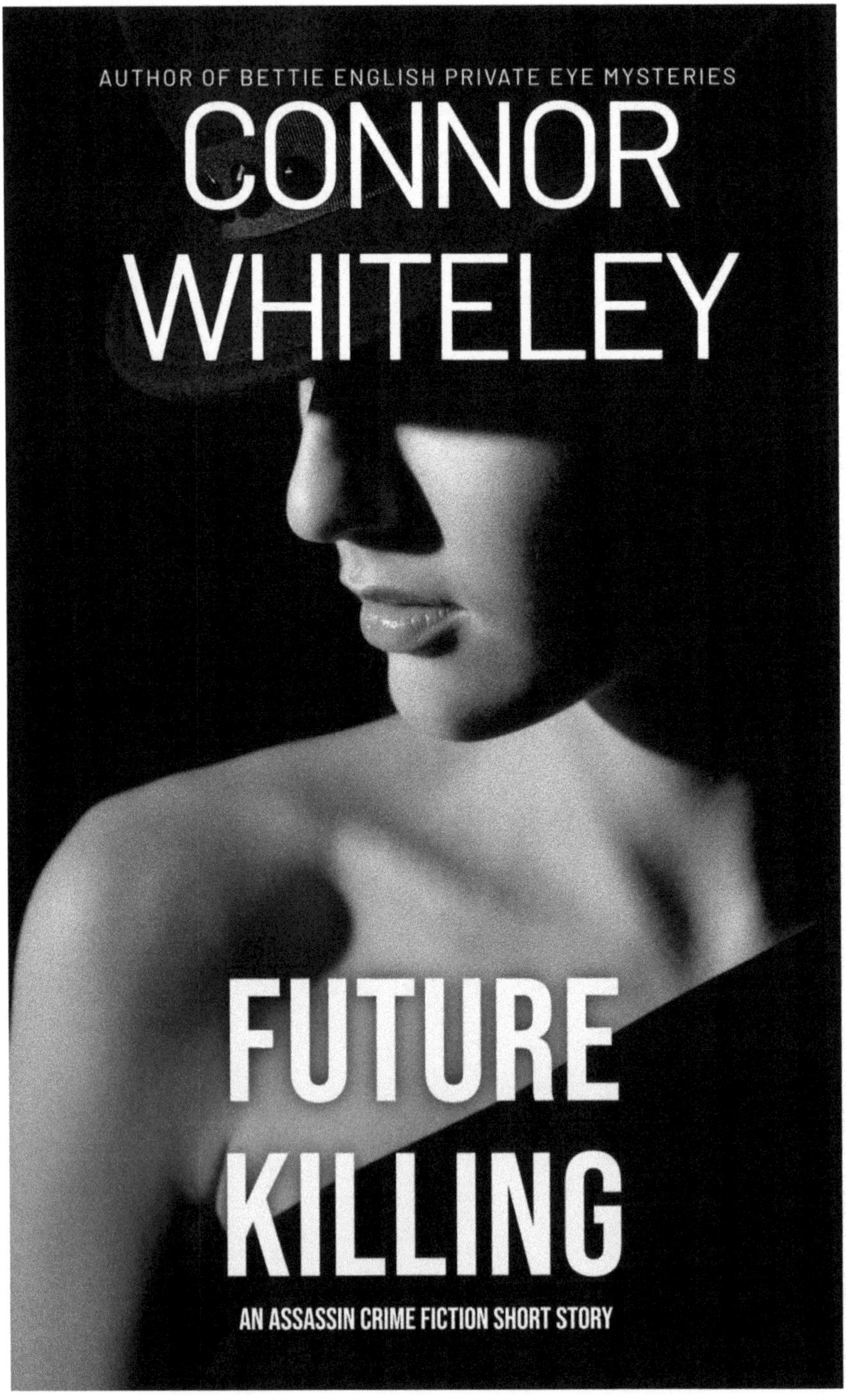
AUTHOR OF BETTIE ENGLISH PRIVATE EYE MYSTERIES
CONNOR WHITELEY
FUTURE KILLING
AN ASSASSIN CRIME FICTION SHORT STORY

FUTURE KILLING

When my father started becoming a professional assassin that was an expert in all ways to kill, dismember and hide corpses, he didn't have even half the tricks that I do today. He used to have to dissolve bodies in acid, use archaic knives and guns and he even had to use his "charm" to help kill his targets.

Thankfully he's long, long dead and because of modern technology, I've been alive for a good hundred or two years and that means I get to enjoy all the new wonders and delights of this modern world as I too take contracts and get paid for killing people.

As I sat at a bright white kitchen island in my London penthouse apartment with immense floor-to-ceiling windows that gave me a 360-degree view of all of central London, and it was so beautiful, I just smiled to myself as I sipped my specialty coffee that I had pinched from a dead guy's kitchen.

I loved how my kitchen smelt so warming and welcoming today with fresh, bitter hints of coffee, crispy bacon and freshly toasted sourdough leaving the best taste of a full-English breakfast on my tongue.

I was sure the delightful smell would pull my girlfriend from my bed in a moment.

In fact most of the things from my apartment came from dead people. My long polished concrete flooring, that idea came from a job involving a lot of acid, some holograms and a holo-rifle where I killed a woman because she was stealing from a charity.

My crystal coffee mugs actually did come from a millionaire's kitchen when I had to kill him for abusing his wife, her friends and his own sex slaves. I seriously enjoyed killing him.

And my favourite thing of all, my little brown hamster called Toby, I rescued from the mouth of a snake of a gangster that I had to kill after he burned down two shops.

So as you can tell I really do like killing people, but I only ever kill people that deserve it and they are criminals themselves. I never kill innocent people, because that is simply monstrous and I am no monster.

You see my name is Grace Bennett, a top-level professional killer that takes brand-new contracts every day from a range of innocent people needing my help to save them. Most of the contracts are weird and just criminals pretending to be innocent but sometimes innocent people need my help.

Like the request I currently had open on my blue holographic laptop.

It turned out that Jennet ShadowLord (clearly a fake name) wanted me to kill her business partner because she was diverting funds towards the middle east and using the business as a front for smuggling things in and out of Iran. Now personally I don't have a problem with money going into the middle east as long as it isn't funding terrorism and anything going into Iran is helping the innocent Iranian people and not the government.

So I checked out what Jennet's business partner was doing with the money and she was very right to be concerned. The advantage of modern technology is that I could easily hack into wherever I wanted to without being traced.

Mrs Zoe King was a great woman on paper. She was kind, helpful, donated ten hours a week to a homeless charity and she did everything a mother was meant to do for her children.

But that was all a lie.

In reality, Mrs Zoe King was a monster. She sent her employees threatening emails ordering them to repay their £20 an hour wages until they only had minimum wage or she would hurt them. Ten employees in the past three months had gone to hospital for "falling downstairs" and another two had died because of "muggings gone wrong". And Mrs Zoe did not have any children, the social media posts used child actors that were paid handsomely and thankfully never touched by her.

Zoe King was a killer. That much was clear and now I had to stop her.

"Good morning babe,"

I grinned as my hot sexy girlfriend, Bella, came into the kitchen wearing an extremely hot, sexy and downright seductive business suit with her amazing blond hair tied up in a bun and she looked ready to work.

"We need to kill Zoe King," I said.

Bella frowned. "I had a hit on her two months ago and I only managed to shoot her in the leg,"

I nodded. I knew Bella wasn't as good as me but no one else actually was. I also knew that Bella wasn't stupid though, if Zoe was still alive then there had to be a very good reason for it.

"She always wears a holographic shield generator that stops everything going through it going faster than a… I don't know," Bella said.

I had to smile at that. I had heard of holographic shield generators becoming more popular and they had only been invented six months ago, but I hated that this was going to become a more and more common problem.

I didn't know how to kill people using them but I had to find out. Not only so I could get paid by Jennet but also so I could tell my fellow assassins.

Sure I could make a hell of a lot more money by being the only assassin able to kill people using shield generators but I was too good of a person to hoard knowledge that powerful.

"I think we need to kill Zoe at home," I said.

Bella nodded. "Okay, I've been to her home before so they

know what I look like but you would be perfect,"

I double-tapped my holographic computer a few times and bought up the small little house that Zoe lived in just outside London. It wasn't exactly the house of a millionaire but that was what made it perfect.

The biggest weakness of posh, rich, evil people was that they always overcomplicated the designs of their big mansions so it was weak. A smaller house meant less entrance points, less gaps and fewer problems for security.

It meant more problems for me.

"There are three guards on the gate. Ten guards in the front and back garden. Another thirty guards inside the house," Bella said.

I just couldn't believe that. Fifty guards for a small house that couldn't possibly fit them all inside. Zoe had to be extremely rich to pay them all but somehow I had to kill them all.

Or not.

"Do you remember how Zoe gets into the house?" I asked.

Bella shook her head so I hacked into local traffic cameras and of course they didn't cover the house. Damn modern technology and how the speed limiters in all cars had meant traffic cameras were useless.

I scanned the internet to see if anyone had ever taken a picture, video or posted about cars or Zoe somewhere getting into her house.

And thankfully it only took me three minutes to find a pro-democracy demonstrator filming Zoe's house and he was shouting at her as she exited her car and went into her house.

The man was shouting about how Zoe was allowing Iran and other corrupt countries to burn instead of letting the people to choose what they wanted.

He died two days later in a "mugging gone wrong".

That got me thinking so I looked at the beautiful love of my life. "Have you ever mugged someone?"

Bella gave me a wicked grin. "Of course I haven't. I would never do such an awful thing and that's a crime. I don't commit crimes,"

I playfully hit over her head and grinned. "We need to get Zoe to a place of our choosing, mug her and kill her so she can't hurt anyone again,"

"What about her criminal empire?"

I gasped. Of course just because we killed Zoe didn't mean that the smuggling would stop, the stealing from Jennet would stop and neither would they abuse the employees were getting. As it was clear that Zoe didn't get her hands dirty.

I double-tapped the holographic computer some more and I started searching for proof about who else was behind it.

Bella grabbed her own red holographic computer and we both started searching.

Within ten minutes we discovered the twenty people under Zoe's command and that was everyone who was involved with her foul conspiracy and as me and my beautiful Bella got to work collecting the evidence and secretly sending it to the police, my mind turned to how we were going to kill Zoe in a very, very fun way.

***

The next day at three o'clock in the morning, I started off my day in the best possible way as I slit the throat of Zoe's normal driver, I put on his clothes and I drove to pick up Zoe at five o'clock.

She was very chatty in the black SUV, she didn't care that her normal driver was sick and I was wearing rather ill-fitting clothes. She didn't even find it weird when I took her down three wrong turns.

And when Bella popped down the seat next to her and zapped Zoe knocking her out cold she didn't even fight back.

"Why can't everyone be this easy?" Bella asked.

I laughed as I disabled the GPS which was so much harder than when my father started professional killing in the early 2010s. Then I simply parked the car in a construction site, torched it and took our guest onto the top of a construction building.

I had given up on my idea about a mugging gone wrong. It would have been poetic justice but I needed a little entertainment this morning and muggings were so boring. Instead I wanted something more artful and creative.

The top of the building was nothing more than a concrete platform with nails, screws and planks of wood just left around for anyone to use or fall over.

Bella the sexy woman that she was had already tied up Zoe and was just about to push her off the top of the building when Zoe awoke just like I planned.

She screamed and screamed and I just enjoyed the sweet scent of lavender, damp and pine that clung to the early morning air. Bella laughed at Zoe but didn't drop her yet.

There were a lot of steel reinforcing rods hundreds of metres below us so whatever happened Zoe was going to get impaled today one way or another.

"Who are you people? How much will my freedom cost?" Zoe asked.

I just shook my head because I hated people like Zoe. To them money was the only answer and it excused everything in her world, whoever had money had the power to do whatever they wanted.

That luck was so running out today.

"Say sorry for all the lives you've taken, beaten and stolen from," I said.

It was a simple question but Zoe laughed at me. "I was just doing what was best for those criminals in Iran. And that pro-democracy crapper was a nutter, he deserved to be in some Iranian Prison and tortured but my clients just wanted him dead,"

I smiled at her. She was clearly evil and at least with her dead and her associates in prison she would never be able to hurt anyone ever again.

I nodded at Bella and she gave Zoe a quick little kiss on the cheek and she let go.

I really wished we had let go together but we would do that on another killing and I just enjoyed listening to the deafening screams of Zoe as she fell and smashed into the steel reinforcing rods below.

Then everything went silent minus the distant sound of her rich dark red blood dripping down on the concrete below.

***

Later that day I was sitting back at my wonderful island just watching and enjoying my hot sexy girlfriend making us a celebratory lunch of eggs, bacon and crispy hash browns. It was an unhealthy lunch so I didn't care we had killed a monster today and if that wasn't a time to eat badly then I didn't want to know what was.

We had had plenty of sex since we returned to celebrate and I just realise how much I loved my girlfriend. She was smart, serious and had an amazing sense of humour when it came to murder and life in general.

And I seriously loved my job, because I wasn't a cold-blooded murderer of an assassin, I was caring and what I did really helped to make the world a better place. Jennet had already paid me, the police had arrested all Zoe's friends and the criminal empire was over.

There would always be more people to kill, more innocents to help and more money to earn but as Bella gave me a smile that melted my assassin heart, I just knew that my life was going to be extremely fun with this stunning woman next to me.

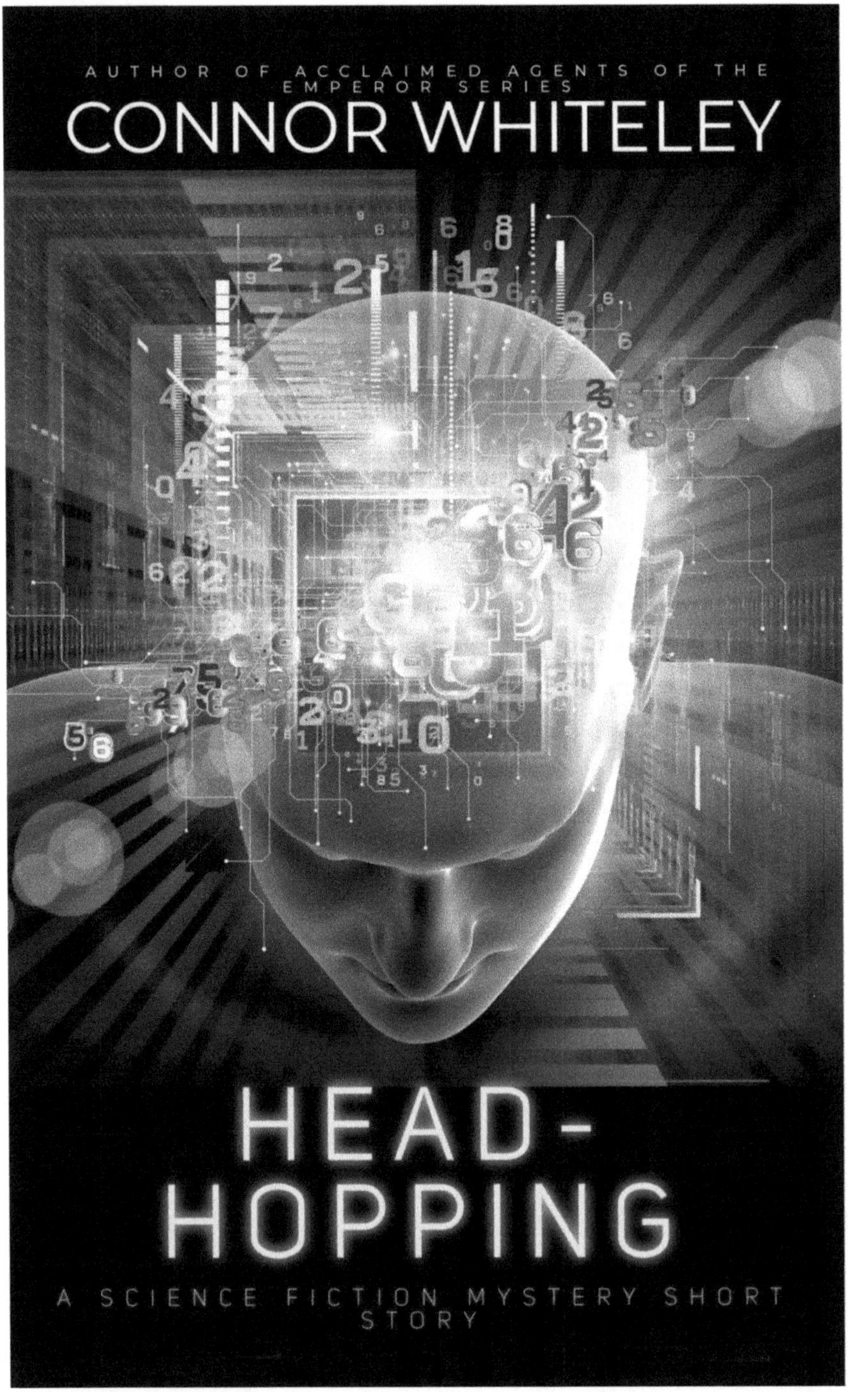
AUTHOR OF ACCLAIMED AGENTS OF THE EMPEROR SERIES
CONNOR WHITELEY
HEAD-HOPPING
A SCIENCE FICTION MYSTERY SHORT STORY

HEAD-HOPPING

Whilst I completely and utterly admit that wanting to jump into the head of a very hot man's girlfriend just so I, Sarah Winter, could admire and get to feel her sexy boyfriend's hard rock body was extremely weird, please rest assured that I am a totally normal woman.

I am a physicist you see by day working for the UK Government on a brand-new piece of technology that allows us to hop into the heads of terrorists so we get to see what they're planning, thinking and fearing so we can counteract their plans.

Then on the weekends I coach my nephew's football team, I volunteer for the local soup kitchen in the evenings and I even give free tutoring to the poor students in my very poor area of London. So yeah, I do a hell of a lot of good and I just wanted, needed to do something bad for a change.

It all started one Friday evening when I was standing in the middle of my bright white sterile lab with nothing even daring to line the edges of the room. It was meant to be a design choice but I know my bosses just didn't want any technology inside in case any cameras got hacked or whatever, and the enemy saw what we were working on.

I wasn't even allowed my phone for eight hours a day. That was a real killer and I couldn't even begin to check my dating profiles, of course they were always empty but it was fun to dream.

The lab was completely sterile and smooth. I hated the too-perfect walls, the freshly polished floor and I hated how the black metal chair with a blue cap in the middle of the lab was the only thing besides me in there.

It was even worse that the air smelt of nothing leaving a dry, musty taste form on my tongue and the sheer silence of the lab was annoying as hell. I needed to do this.

I looked over to my left and weakly smiled at my lab assistant Jerry. He was such a sweet kid, freshly graduated from Oxford but of course just like so many of those posh twats, they were snobs and didn't know anything about the real world.

He was standing behind a large two-way mirror and he activated the mirror so I could see him for now. As soon as I went into the Head Hopper he would change the mirror and monitor the situation.

Of course this wasn't strictly legal but hell, with the UK Government acting how they did these days were laws even more than guidelines these days?

And come on, I had given the best years of my life to this Government (I was 38 after all), this country and this government. I think I deserved just a little illegal head-hopping to see what a relationship could have been like with the man I truly loved at university.

I knew that Jerry was going to try and talk me out of it but he wasn't going to change my mind and I knew my time was limited anyway because as soon as I head-hopped my bosses would be alerted, they would storm in and turn off the machine.

My time inside the head of my target was precious.

"You don't have to do this Doc," Jerry said knowing there was nothing he could do, "the bosses will sack us both,"

I smiled. "You could still bow out and I know you want to do something exciting for a change. Remind me, what has Megan been making you do for the past six months?"

Jerry laughed. "Six months of filing isn't what I studied at Oxford to do. Go ahead Doc,"

I went over to the Head Hopper and sat down, allowing the icy coldness of the metal to fuse to my skin and the blue cap just tightened around me.

"Are you ready?" Jerry asked me. "And remember when your friend's girlfriend's head comes here she will be frightened but her memory will be wiped when you return,"

"Thank you Jerry. I mean it,"

"Good luck Doc," Jerry said as he changed the two-way mirror, the entire room hummed and I finally head-hopped.

But something went wrong.

***

I screamed in pain as I felt like my mind was being shredded up and smashed up with a hammer, this head hop was so much rougher than all the other ones had been and I felt like I was missing something in the back of my mind. Normally I could feel Jerry behind me as he was monitoring my vitals and assessing when to hop me out, but he wasn't there.

I realised I was sitting on the large black three-seater sofa in the middle of someone's living room. The light wooden floors were nice, perfect and freshly polished exactly how I would have had them in my own house.

But this clearly wasn't my house.

The walls were smooth, white and covered in wonderful photos of my university crush and some woman that I didn't know. I just smiled because Caleb Mason really had been the love of my life when I was a university student.

He was always so nice, so calm, so wonderful. And let me just tell you the guy was fucking fit.

He had massive biceps that were noticeable and alluring without being in your face, his body was perfectly sculptured and his legs were so thin and sexy and yeah, all of Caleb was just perfect.

I really did love him, it was just a shame that he had always had a girlfriend when I had known him but the woman in these pictures was different to her.

I went over to a large mirror that hung on the wall over a small black fireplace and realised that I was that girl.

Caleb's new girlfriend in the photos was rather cute I suppose. She was sweet, I ran my fingers through her long brown hair that looked so lustful, beautiful and cute. His girlfriend had a great fit body and I was surprised that I had hopped into her head so well.

But I also couldn't understand why the headhop had been so traumatic too. It was normally so smooth, but I had to admit that I had had one headhop like this before when we were first testing about the programme.

The headhop had been so unsmooth and violent because the woman I had head-hopped into was about to die, and it was the Timestreams trying to stop me from dying inside her body.

I had predicted that if someone died into the head of another person then they died, and the real mind of the victim was alive in the wrong person. It was a nightmare and I really wanted Jerry to find a way to free me.

I heard the front door open and I just grinned like a schoolgirl as I saw my wonderful, sexy boyfriend (Okay not *my* boyfriend I know) Caleb walked in the door holding a large green tarp and a bottle of wine.

He really looked like as stunning and fit and sexy as he had all those years ago. Caleb was just perfect and his smile and slight beard told me everything I needed to know about him.

He hadn't changed a single bit since university.

I went over and kissed him softly on the lips. His soft, velvety lips were just as soft, delicious and sweet as I had always imagined them to be. They were perfect.

This moment was perfect.

"What's the tarp for?" I asked surprised at how high Caleb's girlfriend's voice was.

Caleb smiled. "You know babe I wanted to do something extra special for you tonight,"

I had always noticed whenever Caleb was around one of my girlfriends she had always *bent* over for him, so I presumed he liked it.

I bent over for him slightly.

"Good girl," Caleb said as he kissed me again and again.

Then he grabbed me by the throat. "It is just a shame I'm going to kill you,"

I just looked in horror at him. This was not the man I remembered from university. My Caleb was perfect, kind and sexy.

This Caleb was a monster.

Flashes of arguments. Flashes of violence. Flashes of pain entered my mind as I sensed that his girlfriend was trying to return to her head.

I couldn't allow her to headhop just yet. I needed to save her, I had to stop this sexy monster and I had to save both of us.

I couldn't switch places yet.

"You beat her," I said as bruises I hadn't realised were on his girlfriend's body pulsed up my arm and chest.

Caleb smiled. "Of course I beat you. Did you forget or something?"

I kicked him in-between the legs.

His perfect body didn't even react.

He simply threw me on the sofa and I just stared at him.

I knew that Caleb was way too fit and sexy for me to be able to outrun him, but I was smart, damn smart and that was why I was going to defeat him somehow. I just hadn't figured it out yet.

But the party was over. I wasn't even going to pretend to be his girlfriend anymore.

"Why did you beat her? Even when we were at university you hated beating or violence," I said.

Caleb shook his head and he started laying out the green tarp on the wooden floors. I knew he was going to wrap up my body and somewhat kill me and leave my body to rot.

I couldn't allow him to do that, I couldn't allow yet another one of his girlfriends to die and let's face it, a monster like Caleb didn't exactly suddenly start killing. I think he had always killed even back at university.

That would certainly explain all the girlfriends.

"I asked you a question," I said trying to deepen his girlfriend's voice but failed.

Caleb just looked at me. "Why are you talking about university? You never went to university and I didn't know you back then,"

I smiled and stood up. "That is what you think Caleb and you have not answered my question,"

Caleb came to me. He went to punch me but I simply grabbed his hand. His eyes widened.

"I might not be your girlfriend but I know self-defence and unlike your girlfriend I will not let you hit her,"

Caleb took a few steps back. "Who the hell are you?"

"Sarah Winter,"

Caleb shrugged. "Nice try she's just an ugly woman from uni. I wouldn't have killed her even if she was hot. She was too smart for that,"

"And so what, you kill your girlfriends because they're too dumb?"

Caleb flew at me.

I ducked.

Fists flew.

I rolled across the floor.

Landing on the tarp.

Caleb laughed.

He grabbed an end of the tarp.

I couldn't roll off.

He jumped on me.

Pulling the tarp over my face.

I couldn't breathe.

"I don't care who you are but I will kill you because you are stupid and only smart people get to live,"

I choked on the tarp. I wanted to breathe. I wanted to kill him.

I kicked.

He wasn't moving.

I felt him push his fingers into my mouth. The tarp material felt awful against my tongue.

I chomped on his fingers.

He screamed.

Metallic blood filled my mouth.

Caleb leapt off me.

I flew at him.

Leaping into the air.

Kicking him in the chest.

He fell on the sofa.

Knocking off the wine bottle.

I grabbed it.

Whacking him in the head.

And then I head hopped away.

***

I have to admit that the next twenty-four hours had been rather strange if I do say as a professional head hopper because I had had to explain the entire situation to my boss as this was an illegal operation. Thankfully, I still had my job, security clearance and I wasn't banned from head hopping but my name was officially given to the Murderer team.

So once a week I would have to go into the heads of killers to find out whatever the police wanted, oh fun and believe me that is a serious punishment. I hate the heads of killers and serial killers.

But as I stood back inside Caleb's living room, I had to admit the room felt so much colder, less friendly and deadlier than it had yesterday. I looked at the cute, beautiful woman on the black sofa as she looked unsure at me.

I had no idea why my boss wanted me to speak to the woman I had illegally head-hopped into, as soon as I had knocked on the door she seemed to know everything about me and that annoyed me.

Head hopping was meant to leave me completely protected but this head hop had been weird, because I hadn't been able to access her memories but she might have been able to access all of mine.

I couldn't deny that Caleb had great taste in women because Chloe, as I now knew she was called, was a real stunner. She might have had all her hair tied up in a long ponytail but she was still beautiful and her long flowing blue dress really highlighted her great figure.

"So you're the real woman that head hopped into me?" Chloe asked smiling. "I admit you do have cute nephews,"

I smiled. "Yeah Johnny and Frank are cute, so you could see all of my memories but I couldn't see yours,"

Chloe shrugged as she gestured that I should join her on the sofa. "I'm what a lot of people might call a special woman because you wouldn't really believe, Doctor Sarah Winter, that your team was the only one working on Head Hopping,"

I nodded, I actually had.

"Well it turns out that my team worked out a way to make sure if a Head Hopper was head hopped into, their mind would be useless unless they were in danger," Chloe said.

Well that was a hell of a shocker and I was just glad to know why the head hopping had been so damn rough.

"And before you ask," Chloe said not even daring to look at me, "I didn't defend myself because you know exactly what Caleb was like,"

I weakly smiled at her, because it didn't matter that Caleb was now in prison. He was just a charming, wonderful monster that knew exactly what to say to women (and men) to disarm them, make them do whatever we wanted and I doubted he wouldn't have convinced Chloe after each beating that he would change.

Caleb was a monster and there was never any excuse for hitting anyone, women or men, because abuse in any form was flat out wrong.

"You're safe now and, if you need anything please let me know," I said gesturing that I was going to leave.

She stood up with me and grinned in a way that I hadn't been grinned at in a long, long time. "You know I did see that you were a little *curious* about sex when I was hopped into your head. Are you free for coffee?"

I just smiled at her because she wasn't a bad-looking woman, she was cute and fit and she might not have been as perfect as Caleb but maybe that was exactly what I needed in my life.

And maybe I needed to find love in some other exciting ways, like head hopping, because perfect men were clearly killers, dating apps were useless and it wasn't like I was getting *it* any other way.

So I took Chloe by the arm and just looked forward to a wonderful night of coffee, talking and maybe even a little more. And now I really wished I had seen her memories just so I would know exactly what she liked in a very special department I was more than tempted to explore late into the night.

AUTHOR OF BETTIE ENGLISH PRIVATE EYE MYSTERIES
CONNOR WHITELEY
FUTURE
FASHION
AN DETECTIVE FICTION MYSTERY SHORT STORY

FUTURE FASHION

When Detective Adeline Ford had first seen the body of the young woman she had been summoned to investigate, to say she was shocked had been a serious understatement. The entire hotel dressing room where all the models for some so-called up-and-coming fashion show was exactly what it was meant to be.

Adeline was so, so glad she had given up fashion shows when she was young because she hated the clinically white walls of the dressing room that reflected the bright white lights so perfectly that it highlighted every single flaw of a model's skin, face and dress. There were mirrors everywhere and even now as she stood on the awfully soft white carpet, she still felt so damn self-conscious.

She had almost developed an eating disorder back in her model days and it was next to impossible to avoid the mirrors regardless of how fat or skinny you were. Adeline had always considered herself a fit woman and her boyfriend loved her, but just looking at the mirrors reminded her how she could trim a thin layer of fat here and there and be the so-called perfect model.

Adeline shook the silly ideas away because that was just stupid model thinking and all models thought in dangerous ways that weren't healthy at all. She had loved her therapist for helping her have a healthy relationship with food again after her modelling career, and she only hoped that all these other models here were that lucky.

Sadly Adeline knew a good chunk of these wouldn't be and that was why she hated the fashion and modelling industry. Damn them all.

The dead woman on the ground was fairly fresh according to Ben Ford, her father and medical examiner for Kent, England. He had already completed his checks and he just wanted her okay to remove the body. Yet Adeline wanted a private look around first of all.

The dressing room smelt of lemon, chocolates and sweet caramel leaving a great taste of valentine's day on Adeline's tongue. It was a wonderful taste but in the modelling world it wasn't exactly danger-free.

Adeline hated her own stalkers from her modelling days and she really hoped that the young woman didn't have any.

The woman was clearly stabbed in the chest and even though the blood spray looked like it was meant to cover her face. Someone had wiped away the blood so the woman's young, beautiful face wasn't harmed by the murder.

And it was strange how the young woman was wearing a freshly made long white dress with brand-new holo-implants that made her look like she had wings, a halo and white feathers covering her skin whenever they were activated.

At least that was what the promotion material had said in the hotel lobby.

It was beyond monstrous that someone would kill such a beautiful and innocent young woman. Adeline had to find out who the hell would do this but she knew all too well that modelling was a deadly game.

The young woman was called Penelope Ace and there didn't seem to be a reason to kill her at all. She was brand-new to the circuit so she wasn't a threat to any of the other models. According to her "friends" (no one had friends in the modelling world) she couldn't model so she would be sacked in two months, and she refused to do pills, had sex with the bosses and do extreme exercise.

Adeline really did love the sound of Penelope. It was exactly people like her that they needed in the modelling industry. It was just annoying she would have been sacked in two months (but that was being generous).

Adeline partly wished she was like Penelope at her age.

"Can I remove the body sweetheart?" Ben asked behind her.

Adeline nodded and watched as the techs walked in wearing their strange white canvas suits that were going to be replaced in the next day or two with a new electronic shield thing that still stopped the techs from contaminating the crime scene but didn't require them to wear the strange white suits anymore.

Adeline had no idea how she felt about that modern change, let alone her father.

"Dad," Adeline said, "when can I expect the autopsy please?"

Ben smiled a little. "It will be done when it's done Detective, but I can give you a preliminary analysis in five hours if you want,"

Adeline nodded her thanks and just looked at the mirrors of the dressing room as she couldn't help but feel like she was entering something far darker than she had wanted to admit.

***

The first thing that stuck Adeline as flat out weird about the dressing room and the day was that there were only three people in the entire modelling area of the hotel. There was Penelope of course, the fashion show's director called Molly and a rather hot young man called Arthur.

Adeline had wanted to interview them separately but apparently according to her boss that couldn't happen, because the hotel owner had already called the Police Commissioner who had called Adeline's boss. The top-brass wanted the case solved yesterday.

As much as Adeline hated the endless power plays in the modelling world and how that interacted with the police (something that never should have happened), she had caved and gathered the two remaining suspects in a stunning conference room.

The glass domed walls of the conference room were so much better than the horrible mirrors of the dressing room. The room smelt normal of sweat, orange-scented cleaning chemicals and a subtle undertone of honey for some reason. Adeline really did appreciate the normal aroma after the strange loved-up smells of the dressing room.

There was a large conference table in the middle made from wood that Adeline wasn't a big fan of it, but it would do the trick perfectly.

"What's the meaning of this?" Arthur asked.

Adeline just looked at the hot young man who was sitting perfectly straight on a small chair that made him seem taller than he actually was.

As a fashion worker or maybe designer (Adeline hardly cared enough to check her notes) she expected him to wear top-designer clothes or something so weird it would scream fashion designer. But he looked normal in a white t-shirt and jeans.

It was shocking to see someone normal in the modelling world to say the least.

"This is a murder investigation," Adeline said, "and I want to ask you two some questions. I've checked security cameras and you know you two were the only people in the area today. One of you two is the killer,"

Both Molly and Arthur looked at each other in horror right on cue.

Adeline had to admit Molly with her massive floppy holographic hat, immense eyelashes and ugly dress, fit what Adeline imagined of the fashion industry a lot more.

Adeline remembered Molly from her own modelling days and Molly had been a good model so the magazines had said, but clearly all the plastic surgeries, drugs and dieting had taken their toll on her. Molly never would have been looked at as a model these days.

She might have looked a normal healthy weight by today's standards but as a model she was easily four stone too heavy.

"I remember you," Molly said frowning. "I read a gossip piece about you twenty years ago about you exposing your promoter for pumping pills to you all,"

Adeline didn't actually think anyone had read that article.

"You ruined a lot of good lives you did," Molly said. "I was meant to appear in one of Benson's shows two months later. I could have still been a model today if you hadn't had grown a spine,"

Adeline smiled. She hadn't remembered her old promoter's name for the past twenty years and she really didn't have the heart to tell Molly there was no chance she would have been a model today.

"Why did one of your kill Penelope?" Adeline asked.

There was no forensic evidence and until the autopsy came back she didn't have much to go on.

"We didn't," they both said a little too quickly for her liking.

Adeline stared at Molly. "Penelope was well-known for being against pills, extreme dieting and exercise. I know you are a strong supporter of that lifestyle. What if I told you Penelope was writing an article to expose you?"

It was a lie but Adeline wanted to watch her reaction.

"Then the joke would be on her detective," Molly said. "I *may* be a pill-pusher and I *may* heavily support my models going to the gym for two hours a day no matter what, but I was paying Penelope a thousand pound sterling a week so she was quiet,"

Adeline nodded.

Arthur leant forward. "Exactly and she told me she was donating it every week to eating disorder charities,"

Adeline was amazed at this young woman, she really was incredible. If Adeline had had an extra £1,000 a week at her age she certainly wouldn't be donating it to charity.

"Stupid woman. There's no such thing as eating disorders. There's only thinness," Molly said.

Adeline was so going to get a search warrant later on to search Molly's hotel room and home for drugs. Molly was a danger to the life of her models.

Then Adeline looked at Arthur. "Why would she tell you what she was donating her money to? It makes no sense unless you were closer than you learnt my patrol cops to believe,"

Arthur looked at the ground. "I didn't kill her okay,"

Adeline went over to him. "You're going to have to do better than that,"

Then Adeline moved herself so she could also see Molly's reaction to whatever Arthur was about to reveal.

"Six months ago we were doing a show in New York to launch our new holo-range of clothing. Penelope was attacked by a group of men and they wanted to have *fun* with her so I saved her. We talked, had fun and we had sex that night,"

Adeline nodded. She could see where this was going.

"You're fired," Molly said. "You cannot be sleeping with *my* models you little creep,"

Adeline shot her a warning look. Molly was a foul old woman that needed to be locked up.

"We had sex every night after that and she proposed to me three nights ago. I said no because I knew Molly would have fired us both. Penelope was braver than me, she didn't care,"

"Stupid boy," Molly said.

Adeline really wished she had something to throw at the damn woman.

"Penelope was upset so she ran away and that was the last time I really spoke to her. All I got after that were a few hellos and goodbyes after work," Arthur said.

Adeline just looked at Molly as she grinned like a little schoolgirl at seeing Arthur in pain.

"You killed her," Adeline said, "and I know why,"

Adeline was amazed she hadn't seen it sooner but the key was always the mirrors and the strangeness, perverseness of the fashion industry.

"You're a textbook show director. You push pills, you push eating disorders onto your models and you do every trick in the book to control them. You even cover the dressing room in mirrors so they know exactly how "too fat" they are,"

Molly grinned like this was all perfectly normal and acceptable.

Adeline frowned. "I bet you even film them. You bought special mirrors that allow you to put a camera behind them so you can record them whilst they change,"

Molly grinned even more.

"I'm guessing Penelope came to you the day after Arthur refused to marry her because he was scared you would fire him. She came to you wanting your word you wouldn't find him. No, she was too smart for that. She wanted it in writing,"

Molly grinned a little less.

"You said no of course then Penelope threatened to expose you. She didn't care about the £1000, she only wanted the man she loved,"

"Of course I killed her," Molly said. "The little bitch left me no choice. I mentioned that I had footage of her naked body, I even had a sex tape on her and Arthur. But the little dumb bitch wanted to expose *me* anyway,"

Adeline so badly hoped Molly would rot in hell for this.

"But you know what detective. All these models come through my doors all high and mighty but they know what they're getting involved in. They know in the modelling industry they're nothing but pieces of flesh to be sexualised, objectified and moulded into my image. They don't care as long as they're having fun. But annoy one of those sluts just a little then they are outraged. It is the models that are the criminals, sluts and bitches here. Not me,"

Adeline just laughed. Partly because she could see the truth in her dark words but also because she was so excited about arresting Molly and searching her house for drugs.

Whatever happened next Molly was going down and that was a promise.

***

Two days later, Adeline wore a very smart, black suit and stood outside the large brown doors of a courtroom, and she was actually surprised that her heart wasn't pounding in her chest like it always did just before court. The long sweeping white marble corridor was very empty compared to normal and that only excited Adeline even more.

The corridor smelt of apples, oranges and strong bitter coffee, and after the past few days that was such a familiar and wonderful smell. It smelt like home. There was a very tall male lawyer in a black silk suit walking about, and Adeline was glad she felt at home here.

She hadn't realised it until this particular case how strange the modelling world was and why she was so glad she had put it all behind her. She wasn't a model anymore, she was a detective, investigating crimes and hopefully getting justice for the victims that never deserved to die.

The past two days had involved a massive search of Molly's hotel room, home and even her family estate that she often visited. The judge was thankfully persuaded enough by Molly's own callous words about models that the judge didn't care what was searched to be honest.

Adeline was still amazed they had found thousands of pounds worth of dieting pills and all sorts of drugs, sex tapes and illegal footage. She knew that Molly was going to get a Whole Life Sentence for her crimes and that made her extremely happy.

Molly was a danger to the world, to women and everything that the modelling world should be working towards. Thankfully Adeline had already persuaded Arthur to take over the model shows from Molly and he had agreed, so maybe things could improve for those models, but that was the dangerous thing about the fashion industry. No one was safe from its predations and it wasn't hard to get corrupted by its powerful players.

Adeline had almost fallen off that cliff before.

As the large courtroom doors opened and she was summoned inside, Adeline just grinned because she had to present her evidence and she was going to make sure there was no way in hell Molly was going to escape this one.

Adeline had to do it for herself because of her past, the models Molly had ruined and poor brave Penelope that had done the impossible and fought against an industry that ultimately killed her.

AUTHOR OF WAY OF THE ODYSSEY SERIES
CONNOR WHITELEY
ENDLESS
CORRIDORS
A TWISTED DETECTIVE MYSTERY
SHORT STORY

ENDLESS CORRIDORS

Retired detective Audrey Burns had always loved mysteries, murders and puzzles that were often way too complex to her peers at the police that she often solved them before anyone else. She might have hated retirement, but at least she got to have a great few years with her husband Michael as they travelled, sang and danced the years away, before he died of a stroke three years ago.

Audrey had investigated a whole bunch of crimes and mysteries since then using her police background to help people, get justice for victims and to help make the world a better space.

But even she knew this would be her last ever case because she was going to die today.

Juliet Rose, Roy Davenport and Ben Lloyd were just three of the people that had disappeared from the Rosey Gold Hotel in southeast England over the past decade. Over a hundred people had come into the hotel, check-in and then they were never seen again.

From the outside the hotel looked warm, welcoming and inviting but Audrey suspected it was just some kind of weird look to lure in victims that were never going to be seen again.

She didn't really think they were being murdered, because it just had to be impossible to hide that many bodies over the years but something was clearly going on and that was what she wanted to find out.

Audrey went into a large hotel lobby with dirty marble walls that was large enough to fit twenty to fifty people depending on their size.

There was a group of young mothers with babies and young kids sitting in a corner, there was another group standing around a water cooler in another corner with blue hats and jeans, and then there was only one other person here.

The woman behind the desk.

She might have had frown lines as big as they came but she looked friendly enough. The entire lobby seemed a little sad and lonely to Audrey and if this was an official police case she would have wanted her juniors to search the entire hotel bottom up in search of any missing people.

There were two large golden lifts that looked like they went straight up into the heart of the hotel, and they were beautiful lifts. There was a strange kind of pitting on the golden metal trims that added such texture and depth to it that it seemed to lift the simple design to a whole new level.

Audrey knew her husband never appreciated her taste in interior design but he did love her. He probably would have hated the lobby and she did too, but at least she could see what the designer was attempting back in the day.

The lobby was large enough for a small café or something to make the lobby less depressing, cold and dirty. Clearly that vision never materialised.

"Can I help you?" the woman asked.

Audrey went over to the desk and smiled at the woman. The woman looked like she was trying to smile but it looked so forced and twisted that it was almost scary.

"I'm here to check out the hotel please," Audrey said. "I want to investigate the disappearances,"

Normally Audrey would have tried to actually pose as a guest, come up with a better excuse or simply pretend to be a private investigator. But every single fibre of her being was telling her she was going to die on this case, so what was the point?

The woman frowned. "You're going to disappear if you go up there? I don't allow anyone there. The only reason we're still open is because my boss owns thousands of hotels across the UK and he sinks money into this one as a tax avoidance thing,"

At least she was honest and Audrey could understand her. The woman was clearly frightened but it was weird how she sounded like she was going to cave.

"Why do you still work here?" Audrey asked.

The woman grinned a little and Audrey could have sworn that her face flickered like a bad hologram for a moment but then it went back to normal.

"I have nowhere else to go and you see all those parents and other people in the corners, they're good people," the woman said.

Audrey shrugged, maybe that was fair enough and maybe they had their own reasons for being in there and not outside in the real, exciting world.

"Just a quick look," Audrey said, knowing that this place was weird to its core and she had to find out what was happening.

The woman frowned. "Fine,"

One of the golden lifts opened its doors and a light breeze with hints of salt, rosemary and roasted lamb filled the air pulling Audrey towards the lift. It was weird.

Audrey checked that her holo-phone was on full-battery and she looked through the large glass doors out onto the sunny street outside. With young happy families laughing, talking and playing in the street, there were even young couples kissing and walking hand-in-hand outside, and the outside world was happy and not in danger.

But this hotel only stunk of danger, death and deceit.

Audrey just had to find out why.

***

As soon as Audrey stepped out of the golden lift and the doors shut firmly behind her, she knew she was in deep, deep trouble. The long endlessly white corridor looked so vast that it could have stretched on for hundreds of miles.

It was flat out impossible for such a thing to exist but the hotel was weird. The corridor smelt pleasant of sweet sugar, caramel and male deodorant just like Michael used to wear. The corridor was long, narrow and every two metres two brown fire doors appeared.

Maybe the original design of the hotel was so hundreds or thousands of people could stay in the hotel at any one time. It was so massive that it seemed possible, too possible actually.

Audrey wasn't a fan of the dark orange carpet or the dark flickering lights that were embedded in the ceiling, but she had to get answers.

She started walking down the long corridor and she had to admit she had no idea how she was going to get answers. If no one was up here except the missing people then she couldn't talk to other people to find out what happened.

She didn't have access to a forensic team or dogs or anything that she used to in the police to help her solve cases. She was all alone, vulnerable and she was going to die.

After a few minutes of walking, Audrey stopped and looked around and she couldn't believe that she was only five doors away from the lift. She might have been an old lady but she wasn't slow, she easily caught up with her grandchildren who were all on sport scholarships.

She easily should have walked the entire length of the corridor in those few minutes.

Audrey kept on walking, tapping on the hotel doors as she went and she could have sworn that sometimes her hands fell through the doors and into a coldness like no other on the other side.

As much as Audrey just wanted to escape now, she couldn't. There were at least three different people that might be alive and might need her help.

So Audrey just kept walking back the long, narrow perfectly straight corridor. Passing brown hotel doors along the way one after the other, one after the other.

She kept walking and she looked at her watch and it had stopped. Her watch was nothing special granted, it was just a cheap thing that Michael had bought her one birthday as a joke present to hide the fact he had booked a trip to Mexico as a surprise.

But in all the twenty years she had had it the watch had never stopped until now.

Audrey stopped walking and realised she was only ten hotel doors away from the lift that she had started out on.

Her heart slowly started to beat faster and faster and the hairs on her neck stood up like soldiers. This wasn't right, it wasn't natural, it certainly shouldn't have happened in a hotel.

Never in her life had Audrey believed in ghosts, monsters or whatever other nonsense the "scary" books that she read her grandkids tried to scare her with. She was a perfectly rational and logical person in a very bad situation.

This couldn't be happening.

Then Audrey checked her phone and it was dead. A brand-new holo-phone that had over a week of battery on it was dead something that never ever happened in this new and modern age.

Audrey's stomach twisted into a painful knot as she realised that this had been a massive mistake. She might have known this case was deadly, risky and twisted as soon as she decided to investigate it, but she should have listened to her gut.

She shouldn't have investigated it.

Audrey had even updated her will, made plans to sell the house and divide up the money equally amongst her grandchildren (her own children were already very rich in her will anyway) and she had written letters and personally given each of her children and friends one so they knew exactly how much she loved them.

Audrey blinked away tears.

And when she opened her eyes again she was in the middle of an endless corridor that stretched on for thousands of miles in both directions. She couldn't see the lift door anymore and she couldn't smell or hear anything.

The entire situation was eerie and she knew exactly what had happened to everyone now. They had been taken by something or someone and now they were doomed to roam the endless corridors of this hotel forever.

Distant cries and screams for help echoed all around her but Audrey couldn't see anyone until a little lost man just like those in the hotel lobby walked up next to her like a ghost, he stopped for a moment and just kept on walking.

Then Audrey felt immensely cold and she realised she was just another victim. Whatever weird technology was behind this hotel, it had just claimed her and it was the woman at the front desk that had to be involved too.

Maybe the woman was a part of the technology and that was why she had flashed earlier. Maybe she was a real victim, and maybe she didn't have a boss at all. Her only purpose in the hotel was simply to lure in guests to become part of the technology and the hotel.

As Audrey set off down the endless corridor in some vain stupid hope to find a method of escape, she simply couldn't believe how stupid she had been and now she was trapped forever in this endless hotel, doomed to walk endlessly and never ever rest in peace.

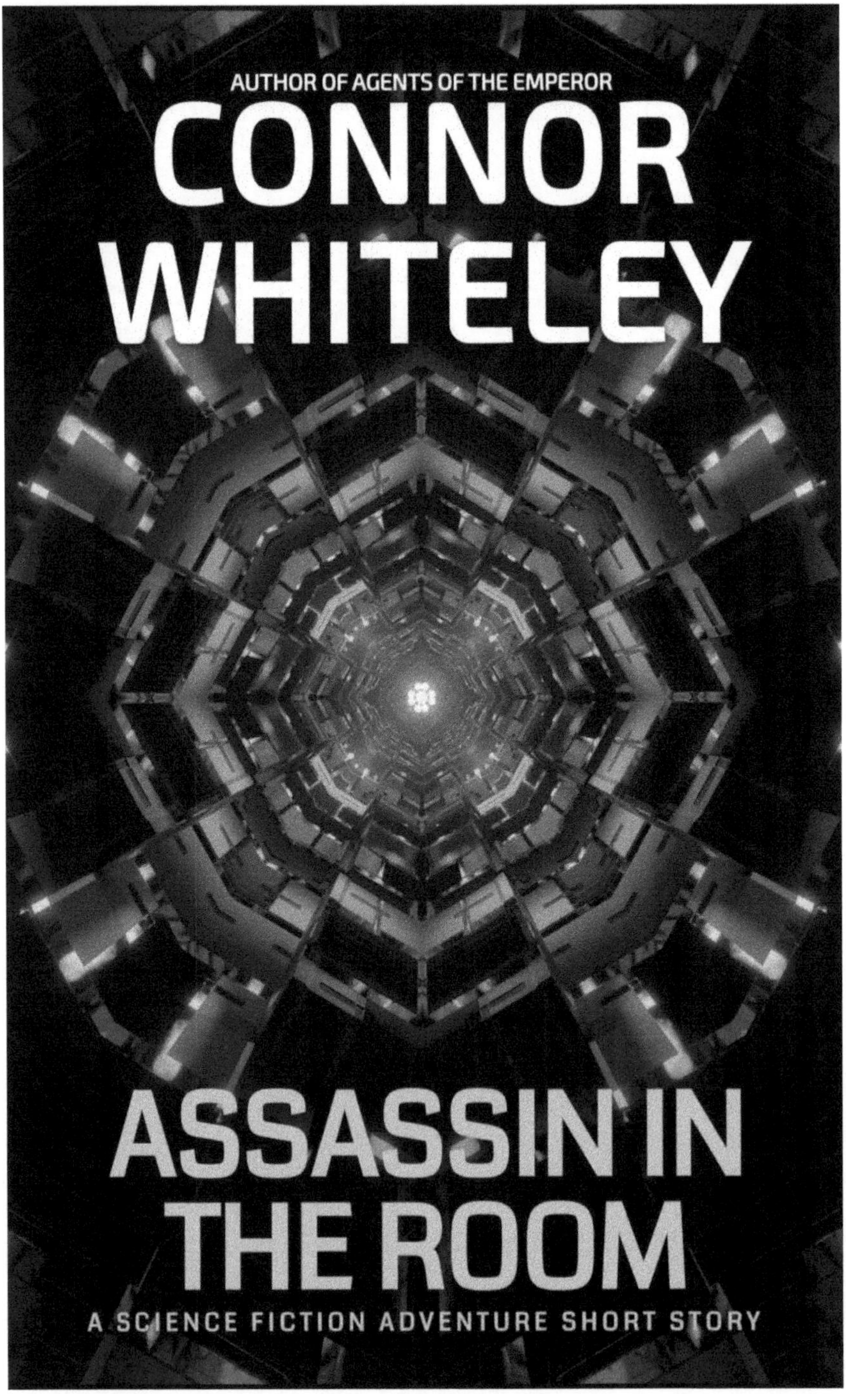
AUTHOR OF AGENTS OF THE EMPEROR
CONNOR
WHITELEY
ASSASSIN IN
THE ROOM
A SCIENCE FICTION ADVENTURE SHORT STORY

ASSASSIN IN THE ROOM

I, Arbiter Carter Murphy, just frowned as I sat down at the very large sterile white round table in the middle of the sealed room. I rather liked the situation I was in even if it was slightly (a lot) outside my comfort zone.

I was in a room trapped with an innocent person and an assassin who were also sitting at the table with me, not that I actually needed to focus on that for now.

The room couldn't have been better and worse at the same time for my task of finding out who the assassin was. The walls were long, huge and made out of bright glowing white plastic that was both bomb-proof and impossible to escape from.

The plastic walls had a slight shine to them that I liked, but the problem was that if you caught the reflecting shine at the wrong angle then it was so bright, blinding and deadly that it would and could blind you for life.

I had heard way too many stories of that happening in imprisonment chambers like this.

There was even a small cut every metre or so. I wasn't entirely sure why the walls had cuts in them, but when I had asked the designer once he had just smiled at me. He didn't want me to know but my guess that was there was some kind of foul containment protocol designed to kill everyone inside if needed.

Something I really hoped I wasn't going to need. I had no intention of dying today.

The sweet flora perfume that clung to the air and left the great taste of orange tarts form on my tongue, made me smile as I looked at the first of my suspects. Madison was a sweet-looking woman wearing a very seductive and cute black dress that made her look deadly, alluring and very seductive.

She had been captured investigating an Empire army base and considering there was an assassin on the loose near the base, the guards believed she might be the one.

I wasn't so sure because her long raven hair was so seductive, she wasn't wearing an assassin suit, she didn't have any weapons and her voice was so calm and relaxing. I just didn't want her to be trouble.

Because once I found the assassin my duty was to kill them.

The next suspect sat to my right and he smiled weakly at me. He was a young man called Finley Atkinson, he didn't look like an assassin, he certainly didn't have the body for the job and his cover was simple enough.

Finley was a farm boy that walked over two miles every single day to deliver fresh meat to the Empire Army soldiers. He wore a sweet dirty pair of holo-clothes and every single instinct was telling me he wasn't an assassin.

In fact this entire situation felt wrong because I had to find out who the assassin was and I was going to struggle doing that without forcing the assassin's hand.

The things I do to save Lord Commanders visiting random Empire Army bases. I don't even get a promotion out of this.

I knew we were inside my black blade-like Arbiter-Class cruiser that allowed me to travel the Great Human Empire solving crime, killing criminals and doing whatever else was required of me to stop the disease of crime from rotting the Empire to its core.

I could barely hear the gentle vibrating, popping and banging of the noisy Arbiters onboard and the engines as they zoomed us towards a random planet that we had orders to investigate but it wasn't my case, so I didn't care.

"What were you doing near the military base?" I asked Madison wanting her to reveal something dark to me.

"I was hiking," she said. "I was just exploring the local area. You see my mother used to serve in the Empire Army so I wanted to meet people like her,"

The problem with that little story was that it was perfect, too perfect. I couldn't check it here and I couldn't even see if her mother was alive or dead, so the mother being in the Empire Army could be a motive or not.

I simply couldn't tell.

"How do we know you aren't the assassin?" Finley asked.

I sat up perfectly straight as I realised what my bosses were actually up to. It was no secret that I had failed in my last two investigations so they must have created some kind of weird test to see if I was still a good Arbiter or not.

They must have grabbed two random people, one of them a real assassin and told all three of us to find out who the assassin was.

"That is true," Madison said her voice sexy and smooth like caramel. "My boss told me if I find the assassin I get a promotion,"

"Exactly," Finley said. "If I find the assassin I finally get to become an Arbiter or a trainee one at that,"

Damn this all to hell. My bosses were playing a dangerous, deadly game with me because both of the suspects were so cold, composed and looked like they were telling the truth perfectly.

I couldn't tell fact from fiction here so I was going to have to be extra clever, and that involved coffee.

I clapped my hands in the air. "Food synthesiser three mugs of coffee in holo-cups,"

Normally I would have just allowed the dark, night black coffee to turn up in China mugs like they always did but if an assassin broke a mug then it would easily become a weapon.

At least the holo-mugs weren't deadly, but I did hate the awful burning sensation I felt whenever I pressed the mug to my lips.

"Why do you want us to drink?" Madison asked grinning at me.

I smiled because I was hoping I was luring her into my trap. "Because an assassin would always have battle damage and that means they might struggle to hold a holo-mug,"

"That's wrong," Finley said. "Assassins have access to some of the most advanced technology in the Empire. Battle damage can be healed as easily as fixing a gun these days,"

I just glared at him but Madison focused on me.

"How do you know that?" I asked as three large mugs of pure black coffee appeared in front of us.

"Because I read and if I am ever going to an Arbiter then I have to be prepared," Finley said.

I wasn't sure if Finley was telling the truth or not because something just wasn't sitting right with me.

"I presume," Madison said. "For us to escape this room we need to kill the assassin and save the innocent person,"

I nodded. She was right and I had to find out who the assassin was and that meant digging deeper into their past. Especially as assassins spent their entire childhood training so their past would be as twisted as their present and future.

I was more than glad I knew tons about the assassins so hopefully I could be smart enough to catch them.

"How did you grow up?" I asked.

"You first," Finley said.

I didn't know if that was an admission that he needed time to think up a convincing lie but I didn't want to argue right now.

"I grew up on my homeworld of Turner Prime in one of the capital's hab-blocks. It was a nice place but there was this stupid neighbour that always wanted to come round and talk to my dad. She was a charming lady but my dad wasn't interested in her advances,"

"That sounds made up," Madison said. "Tell us what you did for fun as a kid,"

"Me and my mates used to go to the old junkyard. We would fix up some speeders, we even fixed up a shuttle once and flew around. The engines popped out ten minutes later, we crashed and spent a week in hospital. Still the best time though,"

My two suspects still didn't seem too convinced, I had always thought of myself as a better liar than that, I would have thought my training had helped with that.

Madison stood up and paced round for a little while. "My childhood was actually spent on Earth right under the Empire Palace, it was beautiful and I had a mother, father and two brothers,"

"What happened to them?" Finley asked.

"All drafted into the Empire Army the moment I turned 18 and then I followed them. I served two tours of duty and I was discharged without a second thought as soon as I got an alien biological weapon that made it impossible for me to walk without aid,"

I looked down at her leg and frowned when I saw it glowing slightly. There were probably some nanobot implants or something that helped her walk.

Yet the assassins also used nanobots to help themselves walk and talk and kill. I should know considering how many times I've used them to heal myself. But if Madison was the assassin then I needed to make sure that I was safe and ready for action.

I downed my rich, wonderfully bitter coffee in a single movement and I allowed the pain of the burning holo-mug to give me strength as I knew I was about to confront an assassin.

Then I realised I needed to hear from Finley first.

"Not a lot to say really. I grew up on a farm, I didn't know my father until my mother told me about him a year ago. No brothers, no sisters and I've spent my entire life at my farm,"

I couldn't believe how hard this was because it was so damn annoying that both of their answers were so vague that they were probably fake.

"You're the assassin," Madison said to me.

I smiled. That had to be the most rubbish I had ever heard in all my life, it was such a lie, such a foul accusation. I was an Arbiter, a hero, a killer of criminals.

"Impossible," I said. "I serve the Emperor and only the Emperor. I am loyal to the Throne and I will always protect the Empire,"

Madison shook her head. "Liar. I have hunted rogue assassins for decades and I know the signs. Even I do not know everything about the assassins and you seemingly do. I saw your reaction to my leg and the merest possibility that I had nanobots, you knew the assassins used them,"

"How?" Finley asked. "How do you know so much?"

I just grinned because these two were just such liars and fools and Empire puppets just falling for whatever their foul, corrupt masters wanted them to believe.

Questioning wasn't heresy as the Arbiters had always called it. Questioning was righteous, it was divine, it was what gave humanity hope.

And it gave me purpose in killing the foul traitors of the Empire.

Then I realised that I was a killer first and foremost and I felt some of my mental conditioning just fall away and I realised that I wasn't an Arbiter, my name was actually Assassin Carter Murphy who went rogue three years ago and has been hunting down high-profile members of the Empire ever since.

All in service of the divine Lord of War that doesn't want to enslave humanity, he only wants to guide humanity towards its potential under his iron fist and finally humanity would rule the stars. Or at least the Lord of War could without the stupidity of the Empire.

I just grinned at my two targets. The job had been simple enough, I was meant to infiltrate the Arbiters so I could learn what I needed to learn about the weaknesses of the Empire and then over time simply eliminate them.

I had always wanted to kill a Lord Commander of the Empire Army so when I was close to a planet that had one, I simply tricked the Planetary Defence Force into believing there was an assassin then I went planetside and killed the target.

Then my mental conditioning returned so I truly believed and acted like a simple Arbiter.

Madison reached for a gun that wasn't by her side.

I flew at her. I didn't need a weapon.

I jumped into the air.

I kicked her in the head.

She was too slow.

Finley charged.

I knocked him out with a single punch.

I went over to Madison as she stood up holding her head.

I whacked her across the face.

She collapsed to the ground.

I gripped her neck.

My muscles tensed.

The bright sterile white walls glowed intensely and my world went black as I collapsed into a sleep without dreams.

***

A few months later I was tied and strapped down with holo-ropes onto a massive white medical bed without any comforts. No pillows, no duvets, no nothing.

I simply stared up at the massive white ceiling above me and I tried to ignore the massive blue holographic helmet over my head that would randomly flash images across my head trying to make me believe in the Empire once more. The Empire was just trying to brainwash me again but that was the thing about the Empire, they could never compete with the brainwashing of the traitors and the divine Lord of War.

I heard nurses, doctors and other patients walk around, laugh and chat about pointless Empire things as I just laid in my room. I think I was alone in my room but I didn't know for sure, my head couldn't move and I just had to focus on the flashing images, hypnotic words and all the other rubbish that the Empire used to try to recondition me.

It was all pointless because one day, maybe not tomorrow,

maybe not next month, maybe not even next year. I would escape from here, I would free my fellow traitors and then I would leave here so I could continue to serve the mighty Lord of War once more.

And I could continue to hunt down the leading heroes of the Empire and once they were all dead, the Lord of War could finally free humanity from its own stupidity but was that tomorrow's problem.

Right now though, I needed to look at some pretty images and at least pretend to be falling to this brainwashing nonsense so I could at least get some pudding tonight.

And then I would be just a little bit stronger and one step closer to my inevitable escape.

AUTHOR OF ACCLAIMED AGENTS OF THE EMPEROR SERIES
CONNOR WHITELEY
THE WEIRDO ON THE STREET
A WHACKY SCIENCE FICTION SHORT STORY

THE WEIRDO ON THE STREET

This was the day I died and I wasn't killed by aliens. That would have been nicer.

I had lived on Birch Road in southeast England for all of my life. My parents had moved here down from up North when they were children, they got sick a few decades later I looked after them like any good son would and then when they died, I moved in.

I never did have time for a wife, a girlfriend or even a cheap hook-up no matter how many hot women wanted to sleep with me. I was always too busy either looking after my parents, getting my journalism degree or working my reporter job for the national papers.

Do I regret any of it? No, not really. I loved my time with my parents, university and my national reporter job but ever since I retired from my national job and joined a local community paper (that surprisingly enough paid a lot better) I started to focus a lot more on the little issues of Strood where Birch Road lived.

There was only ever really one girl I truly regretted not having a relationship with and that was Joanna who lived on the corner. She was beautiful with long sexy legs, a fit body and a perfectly stunning face that I wanted to kiss all day.

Sadly I left things too long and she got married, had a lot of sex apparently and had two kids. That was all in the space of ten years before the poor husband died and sadly I hadn't had time to focus on that beautiful angel again.

But that was what happened in Strood and it was a weird place.

Weird in a sense that I had never ever noticed before.

Sure I always knew that Birch Road was rather unremarkable because all the houses along its long perfectly straight road were different in a good way.

Some houses were large, old and had black mould growing around the windows. Other houses looked modern and proud like my one and then others still looked like the owners were trying to look posh but they were failing miserably. Especially with all the overgrown grass, weeds and bushes covering their drives.

The people were nice enough. There weren't that many punch-ups every week, the kids on the street all got along and they were always shouting, screaming and keeping everyone up at night.

But when I took my local paper job I couldn't understand when I started to notice flashing lights in the night sky. Every single Wednesday night at 2 am there were always bright flashing lights and when everyone got up on Thursday morning it took them two tries to get their cars working.

And whilst Strood was not a posh, expensive place in the slightest. Not everyone had bad cars. A lot of people had the most expensive, newest and poshest cars they could afford and I even saw a Land Rover once or twice (the good Land Rover not the bad cheap ones).

To say I was curious about the flashing lights was a minor understatement. I knew the news of the lights were spreading like wildfire, every single Medway resident wanted to know what they were and even the local nutters had officially set up the Anti-Alien Union or the AAU for short.

Oh yes that was exactly how crazy people from Medway and Strood were at times.

I set out to investigate.

It was a freezing cold night Wednesday night in the middle of January when I finally decided to set out and test my theories. I wanted to prove that it wasn't aliens and I wanted to see where exactly the lights came from.

At the end of Birch Road was a massive circular green on the sloping hill that the road sat on, the air was icy, crisp and damp with a mild undertone of mint from where some idiot had planted mint on the green one year, and now the local council couldn't get rid of it.

I liked the smell as I sat on the icy hard ground brushing my fingers over the frost-covered blades of grass as I waited for the lights to appear.

They would appear in a few moments and I had already set up my camera in front of me. It would be recording the whole time and I had two backup cameras too and an old analogue camera I had "borrowed" from my brother's house because he was into all weird stuff like that.

At least if the lights did knock out the power and stop my modern cameras then maybe the analogue one could help me get the proof I needed.

Two minutes to go.

I had to admit that Birch Road was weird at night because it was as silent as the grave but it was even weirder that there wasn't a single car, lorry or anything on the motorway in the distance. You could always hear the constant humming of the motorway in the distance no matter the time of day.

So why was it silent now?

What was even weirder was that there was one house with lights on Birch Road. It was the house opposite mine and I could have sworn I saw someone standing just under their porch light looking at me.

If it was anyone then it would have been Mr Rogers. A sweet elderly man that always kept to himself, he used to have a wife, two kids and two grandchildren but I don't actually know what happened to them. The wife was wonderful and she was so sweet all the time to everyone. It was a shame that she left, or maybe she disappeared.

I knew that Mr Rogers wasn't exactly an active member of the road and he never cleaned his house judging by the immense streaks of black mould covering the outside of his house, but he was definitely standing under his porch light.

Then the lights appeared all around me.

They weren't there a moment ago and the massive orbs of bright yellow light danced around me for a minute until they just stopped.

I looked over to see where Mr Rodgers was and he wasn't there.

I went to reach for my cameras and the orbs of light absorbed them and crackled even my analogue one was destroyed or devoured.

"Sorry son," Mr Rodgers said emerging from the darkness. "My friends don't like technology which is strange because they are technology,"

All I could do was focused on the weird elderly man that actually looked like he was ageing backwards.

I stood up and realised that I was right. Mr Rogers had always had a beer gut, wrinkles and deep black rings under his eyes. I could have sworn he had less wrinkles today.

"You made a mistake coming out here son," he said. "My friends feast on people like you but don't worry. The process is always painless,"

"Wait," I said not understanding what was happening. "You can't just kill me I need to know what's happening,"

Mr Rogers cocked his head. "What? You think I'm going to kill you? That ain't how this works son,"

He laughed and the orbs of light hummed loudly like they were laughing too.

"What is happening then?" I asked.

The orbs of lights started slowly moving anti-clockwise and they hummed ever so slightly louder like they were now doing something to me. And I noticed that Mr Rogers wasn't entering the circle.

I ran.

I had to get out of the circle.

An orb of light smashed into me.

Pinning me to the ground whilst the others ran around circling me.

Mr Rogers laughed hard like this was some hilarious joke. "They always do this. They always try to run when I am simply trying to improve my life and the life of my species,"

"You're an alien?" I asked really doubting the rumours were true.

"An alien comes from outer space. I have always been here. Watching, learning, eating you sweet little humans and living forever," Mr Rogers said.

My eyes widened in horror.

"Yes son. I have been alive for over ten thousand years and when you little humans developed I liked your form, your abilities, your taste. So I developed these orbs to steal your life and gift it to me,"

I didn't want to believe then I looked down at my hands and realised they were grey, wrinkly and all the joints in my fingers and wrists and elbows ached like I had extreme arthritis or something.

I looked at Mr Rogers's hands and noticed they were that of a teenager whilst the rest of him was decades even a century older.

"That is right son," he said. "You know exactly what is happening and I thank you for investigating and coming out tonight. Normally I have to break into people's houses and steal with their youth when they're asleep with their boyfriends and girlfriends. But you were the perfect target,"

I gulped as I felt my feet, knees and hips flood the rest of my body with crippling pain.

"Why don't you just die?" I asked as breathing became harder and harder.

Mr Rogers shook his head. "You humans assume you and everyone thinks I'm a weirdo so I'm not dangerous. I am just a little old man who is always on this street watching, learning and devouring you poor little humans,"

The orb of light pinning me down popped off me and I shook my head as I tried to force myself up. My body protested and screamed in agony as my bones and joints squeaked like they were rusted together.

Then the orbs of light dimmed and widened the circle so Mr

Rogers could step into it and inspect me.

My mouth dropped as I saw how young he looked. He had long brown hair, perfectly smooth skin and a handsome smile that I was sure any woman would love to indulge in.

"I am a new man for another week and because of your kindness I get to enjoy a few women this week before stealing their youth next Wednesday. I might even start with Joanna on the corner,"

My ancient heart leapt into my throat and I wanted to reach out and grab him and punch him but my ancient joints wouldn't allow me to do that.

In fact I felt my cheeks collapse in on themselves and I simply didn't have the strength to stand anymore.

I collapsed onto the icy cold ground and simply wanted someone to stop Mr Rogers from enjoying a romantic relationship with Joanna and enjoying the sex with her that I had always wanted to enjoy myself.

As the orbs continued circling and I felt my brain and bones and body age more and more I just focused on the memories of Joanna. Her sweet smile, her long sexy legs and her fit body. She would never recognise me now and I hated how my brain was also ageing.

I watched as the orbs of lights disappeared and that just left a very youthful man that I could have sworn was familiar but I couldn't remember his name. Actually I couldn't remember where I was, who I was and where I lived.

The man just laughed at me and slowly helped me up.

"Let's get you back home father," the young man said.

I just nodded and followed the nice young man who had to be my son back into his house and I simply focused on one step at a time because it was all my ancient mind could focus on.

And it was all it could focus on until I died.

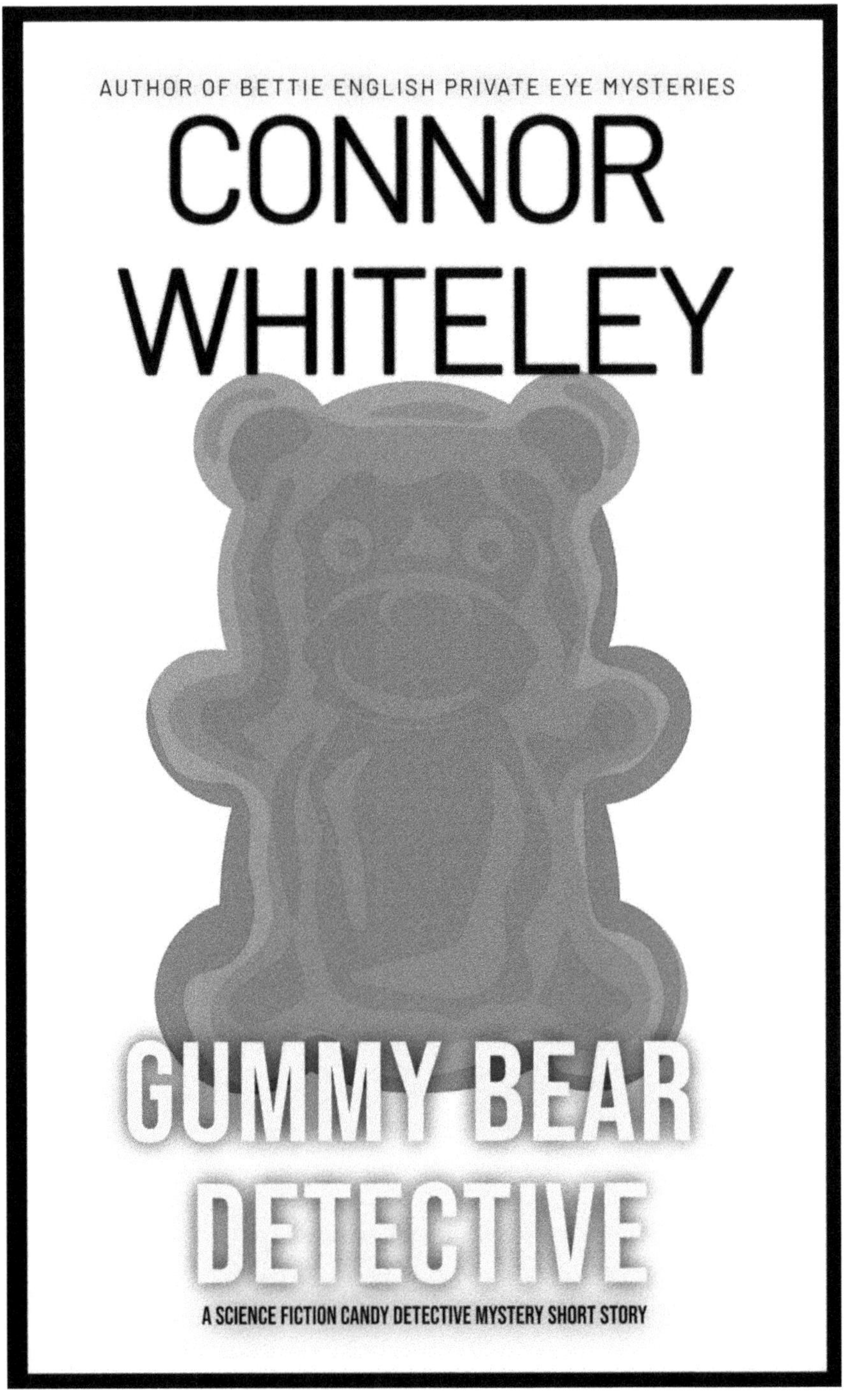
AUTHOR OF BETTIE ENGLISH PRIVATE EYE MYSTERIES
CONNOR WHITELEY
GUMMY BEAR DETECTIVE
A SCIENCE FICTION CANDY DETECTIVE MYSTERY SHORT STORY

GUMMY BEAR DETECTIVE

I never did like Gummy bears before the Candy Awakening, I hated them in fact, to me they never had the delicious taste of chocolate, doughnuts and all the wonderful candies in the world.

So when the Candy Awakening happened which our so-called Glorious leaders did to solve the climate crisis, I wasn't impressed I was some Gummy Bear.

Even worse, I couldn't talk! I love to talk and I can talk for ages, it's something people love about me, I'm wise, clever and I can talk. But for some reason Gummy Bears can't talk, I mean that's ridiculous. I've always been pro climate change argument because we need to save the planet, but I didn't think it would stop my voice.

Just ridiculous!

Anyway as I stare at my large caramel coloured computer made from delicious caramels bits, I tried to see the streams of data pouring onto the liquid chocolate screen but my small gummy bear eyes were tired. I had to have a break.

As I spun around on my black liquorice desk chair and breathed in the sweet cinnamon air that reminded me of cinnamon apple pies from my mother, I smiled at the rest of my friends in the office.

Even I have to admit the Candy Awakening had definitely made my peers more interesting and at least coming to work wasn't the same thing every day. Even coming into the *bullpen* (I still don't know why people call it that) I was always interested in which one of my peers would have a part of themselves chewed off and reshaped today. From licked off toffee arms to melted chocolate legs, we've seen them all.

My small gummy bear eyes narrowed on the rows upon rows of

dark chocolate desks with their caramel computers on as different candy people worked hunched over their desks. Some were writing on milk chocolate slates, others were stacking ice cream folders and others still were doing god knows what.

The sounds of little fingers that sticked to computer keys filled the sweet air as I looked at a large sticky bun that was typing away on his computer. I think he was working on a kidnapping case but I wasn't sure. No one wants to talk to me.

But none of them were gummy bears.

I know what other people say about me, I know I'm a massive three metre tall bright red gummy bear that can't talk. I'm terrifying! I'm something from a children's horror film.

And in all honesty I know some candy people don't even like me, they're scared of me and I fully know that most of these candy cops want me gone as soon as I can.

All because they're scared of me.

But I'm a good cop, I'm a damn good cop. I protect and look after every single candy person I can. Because that's my duty.

Turning my attention away from all my hard working peers and few friends, I looked over at the massive stained glass sugar windows that separated us common Candies with the larger more powerful members of the police. I would love to be one of them.

Those candies were respected, loved and people wouldn't dare hate them. I wish people were like that towards me.

"Daydreaming about ya future again, Frankie Boy?" someone said.

I spun around my liquorice desk chair again and smiled as my only true friend David Alexandria sat down at his dark chocolate desk.

Now I was definitely jealous at the Candy he had become. He was a toffee person! I love toffee but he was my friend so I didn't mind. But for some reason toffee looked good on him, his slim toffee body with his slight muscles looked good and his smooth, slightly shiny toffee hair looked great parted to the left.

A small part of me knew the true reason why I hated being a gummy bear, I hated it because I couldn't tell him how I felt. The worse thing about it all was I was going to tell him I liked him the night of the Candy Awakening but he was busy. So I went to bed and woke up a Gummy Bear.

That was the hardest thing about being a silent Gummy Bear, not being able to tell the man I loved, I loved him.

A part of me knew it was silly to feel like this because how could a toffee man love a gummy bear, but I really did love him. He was gay but my stomach tightened into a knot at the moment of him rejecting me, or worse, not wanting to be my partner anymore.

I couldn't tell him how I felt, at least not yet. Maybe one day far from now, but not today.

Breathing in his sweet toffee scent, I smiled and nodded at David.

"Yea, ya get there one day Frankie Boy," David said.

I really hoped that was true but I doubted it, David knew how much everyone didn't like me but he was hopeful. I appreciated that.

"What ya working on? Any new cases?"

I completely forgot David was about twenty minutes late for his shift and I was working on something before he came in. I wanted to explain how interesting this candy killing had been but I could only point to the report on my computer.

As David came around to look at my caramel computer, I tried not to smile as I felt his warm toffee body pressed against mine.

"Two Gummy Bears killed. Tried to rob a bank. Fight broke out but… their sugar bullets didn't fire. Officers killed them on site," David said.

I nodded and showed him the images of the pistols. In my human life I would have laughed if someone had told me pistols would be made from bright red sugar and still kill people.

It was an interesting new world for sure.

"Yea what ya telling me, Frankie Boy? Tha just normal pistols,"

I rolled my eyes and pointed to the pistols' barrels.

David nodded. "They're brand new. They should have worked, why didn't they, Frankie Boy?"

I shrugged. I didn't know but this was strange, brand new sugar guns should work perfectly. But why didn't these?

"What did tha reports say?" David asked.

A clicked a few buttons and I let him read them. My gummy bear eyes were tired of the computer.

"So both wives said their husbands were acting fine and boring. But the officers noted one of the wives was acting weird. She was crying a lot more than the other,"

I looked at David's beautiful face and shrugged.

"It means Frankie Boy, she could have something to hide. We gonna go and see her,"

David started to walk off with all of his normal stunning confidence but I coughed as the smell of sweet sticky caramel filled the air as I saw a tall Caramel Crime Scene Tech walk over to my desk, placed a small clear sugar box with the pistols inside and gave me a chocolate form to sign. Some nonsense about preserving the chain of custody. Then she left.

David walked back over as I got out the two red sugar pistols that felt rough and heavy in my hands, and handed David the other pistol.

"A little heavy, ain't it?"

I normally didn't want to jump to conclusions until I had held it for a bit longer but I had to agree. Now I had felt sugar pistols a lot in my time, I hated guns and my service weapon but I had still held sugar pistols a lot. None of them were this heavy.

Considering it was made out of sugar, it felt as if it was made from lead. Another ridiculous detail of this case so we have heavy sugar pistols and pistols that won't fire.

"What did ya Crime Scene Techs find?" David asked.

I checked my emails quickly and found an email from the Techs.

As David read it I couldn't understand the email, the Techs said nothing was wrong or strange about the guns themselves. They wondered if these were surviving metal guns from before the Candy Awakening but they weren't. They took samples and were running tests but they weren't hopeful.

Curiouser and curiouser.

I know I haven't been a cop for decades but come on sugar pistols that feel like lead and pistols that don't fire is just plain weird.

Placing the pistols back in the box, I stood up and waved my gummy bear hands at David to come with me, he smiled.

"Where we gonna go, Frankie Boy?"

I wanted to roll my eyes because clearly he'd forgotten I can't talk but it clicked after a few moments.

We needed to have a chat with his wife, I didn't understand what she was so upset about and why the other wife wasn't.

But the deal of talking to upset wives scared me more than I wanted to admit.

***

Whilst beautiful David finished parking our little car made from yellow and red rhubarb and custard sweets (another favourite of mine), I stood outside our target house.

To my relief it wasn't like the strange eerie gingerbread houses from a previous case, it was a rather lovely little stained glass sugar house in the middle of a neighbour made out of chocolate cake.

Sure it looked a little odd with the massive chocolate cake houses and thick mint ice cream road and candyfloss pathways but the house was charming in its own way.

As a human I never liked stained glass sugar cookies where people placed a boiled sweet in the middle and baked it. Revealing a rare breath-taking design in the middle but on a house it looked great.

The entire house was a stunning array of blue, red, green and more colours on the walls made from solid sugar. I hadn't seen anything like it before. (I'm not sure many people had)

The sounds of chocolate cars honking and driving past echoed around the street as they went, and the amazing smell of sweet apples filled the air as I presumed that meant there was a family of apple pie people around here, as I went up to the sugar house and knocked on the door.

A hint of beautiful toffee filled the air as I knew my stunning David with that utterly amazing toffee hair had come back from the car.

After a few moments two Twix bars came out of the house, frowning and their little chocolate caramel arms folded as they came out, pushing me onto the pathway.

I was hardly impressed with these Twix wives, I didn't even know they were going to be together. But these wives hardly seemed friendly and I had a feeling they knew a lot more about their husbands' death than they told us.

The hard way was getting them to tell us.

"What da you want pigs?" the shorter Twix bar said.

I looked at David and rolled my eyes.

As David introduced ourselves and started with the basic questions that we already knew the answer to because of the shooting Officer's report. I remembered what I'd found out about the wives before David arrived.

The taller Twix bar was a posh business woman who ran a

massive international Candy Production factory, which changed to making Candy clothing after the Candy Awakening.

The shorter (and foul) Twix was a nurse in a local hospital who was apparently trying to become a doctor but… I doubted she would ever become one. You have to be kind first!

But what puzzled me was what would bring these two women together, one was kind and successful, the other a foul Twix bar.

"Why ya husbands rob the bank?" David asked.

"I donno pig that's your job, ain't it?"

"Oh honey, please calm down. These two police officers are only doing their jobs like I am,"

My eyes narrowed on the taller Twix.

"Thank you, but ya job?" David asked.

"Oh, please excuse my manners Officer, I am Sarahire O'liea husband to that moron, lawyer and Business Owner,"

My eyes still narrowed on her. I looked on David and nodded, over the years we had managed to create some kind of system so he knew what I roughly wanted to ask.

"What type of law?"

Close enough to what I wanted.

"Oh Officer, it's amazing. I'm an entertainment lawyer with massive connections in Hollywood,"

As the taller Twix went on about her job for a few moments, I tried to understand her and I knew she was lying. How the hell could one person ran a global clothing business and have massive connections in Hollywood and be a massive successful lawyer?

"Ya wanna turn your husbands' deaths into a film?" David asked.

Now I was listening and this was actually starting to make sense. I just couldn't understand the thing about the sugar guns.

"Oh of course Officer, this would be a masterpiece, a blockbuster for the ages, a marvellous creation. Two Candy people rob a bank, but their guns don't work and they die. No cops get hurt, no people, not even the desk clerk that tried to stop them. It would be a comedy for the ages,"

A small part of me couldn't understand how this clearly successful business woman could only see a money making opportunity here. You would have thought she would be at least a little bit sad that her husband (love of her life) was shot dead.

Then another idea hit me so I looked at David and gestured with my hands a desk.

He nodded. "How did you know the desk clerk tried to stop them. That wasn't in the report and it wasn't released to the media,"

The shorter foul Twix took a step closer.

"Ya pigs are useless. Leave us alone!"

The other Twix placed a small chocolatey hand on her friend's shoulder.

"Oh officers, please. The desk clerk is a friend of mine. He called me straight after it happened and he saw the guns didn't work in the slightest. That got my mind going on a film idea,"

Whilst David was completely fixed on what she was saying, my gummy bear eyes narrowed on the shorter woman. She was getting more and more tense with each mention of the guns.

Waving my hands I made a gun sign and pointed it to the shorter Twix. I could see her chocolate sweat starting to drip down her forehead.

David opened his mouth but both our chocolate phones pinged with a message from the Caramel Crime Scene Techs.

I couldn't believe it, the Techs found the guns were Sugotised. I still found the whole sugotising idea extremely weird and just messed up. But it turns out that the same process behind magnetizing something can be applied to sugar objects.

And the shorter Twix worked at a hospital after all.

"Got something ya wanna tell us," David said.

All hate and anger from the shorter Twix melted away as little chocolate caramel tears filled her eyes and dripped down her cheeks.

"Ya pigs are awful. Leave us alone,"

I took a few steps forward and held out my arms.

She backed away. "They were gonna hurt people. Didn't want that. I wasn't gonna let um hurt innocents. I'll be a doctor one day. Doctors don't hurt people,"

I still didn't believe this shorter Twix was ever going to become a doctor but maybe she did have the right attitude.

Again I made the gun signs with my hands and stunning David understood me, one of the few people that did.

"So you took the guns to work and Sugotised them,"

She nodded and I didn't know what to do now, the case was solved, all our questions had been answered but it still felt strange not making an arrest.

I saw David's beautiful little toffee eyes look at me and he too wanted to know what to do. I nodded at him.

"Ya didn't do anything illegal. Ya just protected people, why did ya not call tha police?" David asked.

A good question.

Both Twix just looked at us and we both understood, nothing would have been done, even after the Candy Awakening our police force is stretched too thin. So a random call about a possible robbery, no one would have cared, that was the sad truth of the world, even a candy world.

***

Driving back to the station passing chocolate cake house after house in our amazing rhubarb and custard sweet car, I couldn't help but think about this case and all the questions our Captain would ask about it all. I wasn't even sure how many answers I had for the Cap, the entire case came down to two wives wanting to protect other people while their husbands did something stupid.

I really doubted either wife thought their husbands would die but I don't believe they missed them. From what I gathered the taller Twix loved her work so much she used it to avoid her husband, and the shorter Twix wanted to become a doctor so much she wanted to help people, whilst her husband hurt them.

In my experience those complete polar opposites never work out. But at least now the world might be a little safer and the women might get their stories made into a film, I might go and see it actually.

As I breathed in the amazingly sweet custardy air and felt the smooth sweets press into my gummy bear back, I turned to look at my beautiful David. Just admiring his amazing toffee eyes and that great perfect toffee hair.

If the film ever came out, maybe (No, definitely) I would take David with me, be our first date of sorts.

Knowing the case was over and everything was wrapped up I knew the end of the day was close, so as the car hummed a little more as we changed road types from mint to strawberry ice cream. I knew I had to tell him so when David pulled the candy car to a stop at some lollipop traffic lights, I knew this was the moment.

I tapped him on his soft shoulders and when those stunning toffee eyes looked at me. I made a love heart sign and pointed at him.

As we drove off towards the police station, he smiled.
"I know, Frankie Boy. I love you too,"

AUTHOR OF ACCLAIMED AGENTS OF THE EMPEROR SERIES
CONNOR WHITELEY
GRADUATING IN DEATH
A SCIENCE FICTION CRIME FICTION SHORT STORY

GRADUATING IN DEATH

When I was graduating from the University of Death numbers of years ago, I was actually rather excited, happy and glad that I had done so well on my university journey. Of course, there were plenty of moments when I believed wholeheartedly that I was going to fail my degree and then be killed so I couldn't turn against the glorious Assassin Guild.

There was the moment when I "accidentally" killed an instructor by throwing my knife into her eye despite her wearing goggles. I honestly believed that I was going to get a commendation for that little trick. No, I ended up getting detention.

Then there were the incidents involving me assassinating so-called unauthorised targets. I'm sorry but if a terrorist is within my killing ground then I will always kill them too, because the entire reason why I became an assassin was to save lives, protect the innocent and live an exciting life at the same time.

And the incident with the vibrating dildo and that I killed someone using it, well we simply don't talk about that problem. Regardless of how much I loved the job.

Especially as none of that helps me with my current job.

I was sitting at the back of a massive beautiful cathedral in the south of England. I loved its ancient little gothic architecture that made me feel like I was stepping back into a more primitive time. The pinks, blues and reds of the immense stained glass window was wonderful as the bright sunlight shone through it.

There were tons of great-looking marble coffins lining the sides of the nave filled with so many dead heroes from over a thousand years ago, that I was seriously in my element. I loved the place but then again I do love death a little too much.

The only problem with the cathedral itself was the constant humming, popping and banging of the holo-systems that kept the place from falling apart.

Of course most people had no idea what was above them, but I did. The benefits of being an assassin is that you have to be very up-to-date on your construction material.

I had to focus for a few seconds but the beautiful gothic ceiling above me flickered, moved and looked blurry. That was because of the ceiling had collapsed about two decades ago so instead of "wasting" money to rebuild it, the owner had simply used the new technology to make it look real.

You see I was sitting at the very back of the cathedral because it was graduation day for over three hundred students from the School of Geological Studies. Personally, I couldn't have given a hairy rat's behind about the subject but considering how one of my longest targets had actually come out of hiding to see their daughter graduate, who am I to pass up a great killing opportunity?

"Excuse me," a woman asked.

I gestured that the short woman wearing some kind of black rubber business suit sat down next to me. She seemed nice enough but I knew she would be a problem, because she was now the closest person to the massive wooden doors.

She was blocking my path to escape.

Not that it mattered really because Doctor Frank Selam was my target and he really wasn't a nice man. After the collapse of the United Kingdom, he had become a terrorist for hire, making all sorts of bioweapons and engineering plagues and viruses on a scale the world had never seen before.

Believe it or not that actually isn't enough for someone like me to get called in, but when the Head of United Nations was assassinated three years ago using one of his viruses that was when I was summoned, given a mission and I was now going to complete it.

Of course I had failed a good few times and Francis had repeatedly slipped through my fingers but the Guild hadn't seemed to be too angry at least. They didn't lock me up in a holo-stimulation. I have to admit that I was slightly confused as to why the Guild sent me out after failing a few times but a job was a job.

"Ladies and Gentlemen,"

I looked up at the very front of the university and smiled as I saw the female Chancellor of the university descend like some so-called angel on a hoverboard down from the fake ceiling. She was dressed in ancient robes and she looked awful but she seemed happy.

And considering she was going to be gifting my target an Honourary degree under a false name I was extremely happy too.

"So many people," the woman next to me said.

I nodded and she was completely right. I hadn't had much of a chance to focus on many other people but there had to be over a thousand people crammed into the nave.

There were over three hundred students smiling, laughing and muttering as the Chancellor continued. They were all in their black graduation gowns and holo-boards on their heads. They all looked the same to me so I didn't care too much.

And my target wasn't amongst them.

Then there were another six hundred plus parents and friends and guardians of the students. So many people here just to see their sweet child graduate, it was wonderful really but I wanted my target.

"Tell me," the woman said, "how long do you think it would take to gas all these people?"

I instantly tensed. I actually looked at the woman and I noticed that she wasn't normal, she wasn't right and she certainly wasn't a parent or guardian.

My target was sitting right next to me.

"Relax assassin," Francis said. "I am a master of disguises and the Chancellor is a good friend of mine. She will be just as willing to kill you as I am,"

I shook my head because this was seriously going badly. I didn't doubt for a second that the damn Chancellor had been working with Francis to get me here.

"All I really wanted was to see who was hunting me but look at all these people. Wouldn't it be nice to see them choking and gasping for air?"

"You're sick," I said knowing it would only take one small flick of my wrist to activate my holo-sword but the space was too enclosed. I would probably kill someone, I needed to get him alone.

"Maybe but I think we both know that I am more than capable of killing everyone in this room,"

I looked around and I couldn't believe that he was so cold, heartless and awful towards a thousand people. There were so many happy, smiling and excited young people about the Graduation that I simply could not allow this to happen.

Then the Chancellor started to read out the names of the students as they graduated so they could shake her hand and get their degree certificate.

"What virus do you have today?" I asked wanting to buy myself some time to come up with a plan to get him alone.

"You know assassin I don't actually have one. I sold a virus to someone in this cathedral only yesterday. I have no control whether they release it or not,"

"You monster,"

Francis looked like he was going to get up.

I placed my palm on his chest and flicked my wrist and a holo-sword shot out killing him instantly.

With Francis's dead body next to me I had to find the bastard with the virus as soon as possible. This was bad and I was definitely running out of time because the honourary degree would be issued halfway through the calling out of the names.

And with Francis now unable to get the degree that would signal to the virus user that something was wrong and they would certainly release the virus at that point.

Killing everyone in the process.

I subtly searched Francis's pockets and managed to find his communication bead but then I noticed that a young student was looking at me like I was a criminal.

I simply pretended to make out with Francis and that seemed to make the student think he was still alive. The idiot.

As I placed the holo-bead in my pocket and activated it, I smiled as streams upon streams of data appeared in front of me so only I could see it.

I checked Francis's hail logs and noticed there were no calls for the past week, no emails and most importantly no bank deposits for the past month.

Then the screen flashed and Francis's face appeared.

"This is an unauthorised access of my bead so I must assume that I am dead. The person with my virus will be notified in a few minutes and then everyone will die including you,"

I shook my head and simply deleted Francis's ugly face off the holographic screens until I noticed there was something in the background of the message.

I reinstated the warning and noticed that Francis was in a garden with a hell of a lot of Deadly Nightshade behind him. I have to admit it was old school as hell and there were a lot more sophisticated and untraceable ways to kill people these days.

Then again, Francis had never really been one for covering his tracks. He had always believed he was unkillable.

I was glad to prove him wrong.

But Deadly Nightshade had been used a lot at the university graduation tonight to show how something as old and dull as that ancient poison could be given new life by modern technology.

I had read tons of reports lately about how poisons were being genetically modified, vapourised and mutilated beyond recognition. So I actually believed my real target was a student.

A student that was graduating today because a student working in Geological Sciences did cover Deadly Nightshade, the environments it grew in and how human activity had caused the plant to adapt in recent decades. Then it wouldn't be hard for them to order Francis to adapt it even worse.

And if the expensive and posh clothes the parents were wearing were hardly suggesting there was a shortage of cash in the student population.

I had to find the student now.

I stood up and I was about to break every single assassin rule in the book.

"Stop!" I shouted at the Chancellor. "There is a virus in this area and everyone is about to die,"

No one looked at me. No one spoke to me. No one even tried to stop me.

Then I realised that everyone was flickering, buffing and crackling like a very, very bad hologram.

Then one by one by one the little students and parents and friends all started to disappear. Even the Chancellor seemed to smile at me before she disappeared and then I was all alone in a cathedral.

Until the cathedral melted around me leaving me in a cold, isolated white place. There was nothing but whiteness for as far as I could see and the sheer silence was scary as hell.

I hated the silence, I hated the graduation and I hated Francis Selam because I knew this was a setup.

"It is amazing really isn't it?" Francis said even though I couldn't see him. "You can drug an assassin, you can threaten to kill them and then you can contact the Guild for ransom,"

I felt someone run a finger down my left arm but I couldn't see who was doing it so I had to be in some kind of simulation designed by Francis himself.

"I didn't expect you to trigger my alert systems. I was just about ready to finish up a new virus to gift you when my computers told me you weren't playing along anymore,"

I couldn't believe how stupid Francis was being, he actually believed assassins played by the rules. He actually believed I was a normal person that could be predictable and he actually believed I wasn't going to kill him.

That was true. I wasn't going to kill him. I was now going to gut him alive.

"What do you do?" I asked looking around for a weak point in the simulation. It was a basic assassin trick the Guild taught us all in case this ever happened.

Find the weak point, break the simulation.

"You can try to find the weak point all you want but you will fail. Like you failed to detect me when I broke into your house,"

I smiled. Francis really was a fool because I lived alone, my neighbours believed I was on a business trip for the week and no one would disrupt me.

But I was at home, in my house and I was probably still lying in my bed. I doubted Francis had the balls to actually move me after he put the device on my head meaning I knew the layout of the entire real world outside the simulation.

Including where Francis was standing in order to touch my left arm.

I thrusted out my hands.

And I felt nothing but icy coldness. Clearly the simulation was better than I imagined because I wasn't moving in the real world no matter how badly I wanted to.

"Dearest assassin my little virus is complete now so be ready to be filled with joyous death,"

I forced my heart rate not to spike because I didn't want the virus to go through my bloodstream any faster than necessary.

I looked around. I really looked. I had to find the weak point.

As I hissed in pain as the needle went into my wrist my vision blurred. My stomach tightened. And I saw it.

All the bright whiteness of the landscape buzzed and I saw straight through it and the simulation was clearly struggling to adapt to the change the virus was causing inside my body.

I punched the air.

Smashing into the glass.

I punched again.

Again.

Again.

The glass shattered.

My eyes opened.

I saw Francis's eyes widen as he noticed me and I ripped the needle out of my wrist, leapt up and rammed it into his neck.

Francis tried to move away but he was too slow and I was an assassin.

Pure inky black liquid pulsed into his neck and all his veins, arteries and vital organs turned black as the virus killed him.

As Francis collapsed to the ground I snapped his neck for good measure and then I called in the Guild. They were going to need a full report on this and I already had a sinking feeling that I was going to need a hell of a lot of medical care to fix whatever drops of virus Francis had infected me with.

***

Even I will admit whatever Francis clearly lacked in his ability to move, escape me and create a good simulation, he really did make up for in his craft of virus-making. It had taken twenty world-leading doctors, three blood transfusions and me drinking more water than I had done in my life to save me.

So I walked back into the cathedral identical to the simulation with the awful Chancellor reading out the names again and again as each student from the School of Geological Sciences got their degrees, I simply activated my holo-sword and I was going to get revenge no matter what.

All the students in their gowns and holo-boards looked at me like I was a curiosity, like how I imagined they saw rocks, and all the parents frowned at me. But I loved the look of horror on the Chancellor's face as she saw that I was alive and that look confirmed everything.

Me and my assassin team had researched the Chancellor for two days before we were confident enough to order an assassination on her. Which was granted ten seconds later.

She was as corrupt, evil and abusive as Francis was and it made sense because she was his lover. And she had helped him create the virus that tried to kill me and had actually killed Francis.

Thankfully there were no other viruses on the loose so I just went up the long nave towards the Chancellor as she struggled to say the next name of the next graduate.

Then I stopped in front of her and grinned. "Chancellor Harris you have been found guilty of terrorism, bio-manipulation for malice purposes and occlusion with a terrorist,"

"No," she said.

"You have been sentenced to death by the Guild and your life is forfeit,"

I flicked my sword and the Chancellor screamed in agony as I slashed her neck and dark red rich blood splattered up the cathedral walls and onto the gowns of the next to-graduate students.

"Congratulations on your degrees everyone," I said.

And then I simply left because the Chancellor was dead and the terrorist was dead. I had saved a lot of lives today and now a lot less people would suffer at the hands of crazy people like Francis and his twisted lover.

And most importantly I was alive, happy and free to keep on killing and helping to make the world a safer, better place one death at a time.

In fact, you might even say today I was graduating in death.

CONNOR
WHITELEY
WHAT CANDIES
FEAR
A SCIENCE FICTION CANDY DETECTIVE MYSTERY SHORT STORY

WHAT CANDIES FEAR

When the world was dying, the sea levels rose so high, drowning millions, destroying entire regions, and so the climate emergency was realised. Decades of denial disappeared in days.

I still can't understand why the so-called glorious leaders of the world unleashed the wave that night. Turning us all to candy and sweets and biscuits, but they did.

As a detective that loves cold cases it was partly a dream come true, but it wasn't. It never was, I would be perfectly happy if I was fired because there were no more missing people and cold cases to solve. I really would have loved that.

Just the idea of laying on a sunbed in the middle of nowhere made me smile, no more missing people, no more cold cases, I could happily live in that reality.

That is not what happened.

When the wave was unleashed and the world turned to candy, so many people disappeared, so many were gone, so many lives destroyed.

A part of me hated it at first, I was so mad at all of them. How dare these world leaders do this, how dare they destroy so many lives, how… I knew none of that would help so I channelled my drive and passion into the only thing that mattered.

Finding people.

Which led me to the middle of London. As I stood there, pressing my soft chocolate bar back against a delicious white nougat tree, my eyes narrowed on all the brown dark chocolate gravestones.

There were too many. In all honesty I couldn't understand why the graveyard was so full, all the chocolate gravestones looked like they were piled on top of each other, some were cracked, some were chipped, all were unloved and forgotten.

And that was the sad truth of missing people, no one really cared about them, no one saw them as important. But I did. At least I tried my hardest.

As I breathed in the amazing honeycomb scented air, I tasted the scrumptious honey. Even before I turned into a chocolate bar, I had loved honey, be it honey cakes, raw honey, honeycomb. I loved it all. It was just a massive shame that I couldn't eat it now.

The sound of cars in the far distance echoed around the little square the graveyard was in with large abandoned solid caramel buildings lining it. I had thought it'd be great fun to explore them later, then I remembered how hot it got at midday. I wasn't risking falling through soft caramel floors for no one's love or money.

When someone moaned a few metres from me, I looked along the makeshift strawberry lace grass that had been whipped into some sort of path to see the Caramel Crime Scene Techs.

A small smile broke my face as I saw the Techs worrying about a shattered chocolate gravestone. I wanted to say it hardly mattered, we were probably the first people to be in here for two decades, but it wouldn't have helped. It wouldn't have helped me anyway. As I cast my mind back, I focused on why we were here.

Alexis Stormy was not the type of girl you forget easily. I had learnt that very early on so when she didn't turn up for a party in Soho with her friends, needless to say people were worried and the fact she had so many friends, well, the police got a lot of phone calls.

The police talked to all her friends from what I could see, they interviewed several suspects, an ex-boyfriend, a few bartenders but there was nothing. Compared to most of the cold cases I look at, this one was almost perfect. Almost.

When the case went cold, it was boxed up, shipped into storage and forgotten about because (sadly) who cares about some girl who can't be found. Especially when there were more *important* cases to solve.

I never had liked that attitude, everyone was important to someone. Alexis was important to her friends and her now-dead mother, who died never knowing what happened to her "Little Bundle of Joy". I had to find her.

I focused back on the Caramel Techs who were all holding some kind of metal detector thing made from toffee. I had no idea if that scanner/ detector would pick up anything now, but I had seen stranger things.

After I got the case last week I had read through it all but the police didn't look at one thing. Alexi Stormy worked as a make-up artist for the dead and she was working before the party, she loved her job strangely enough, and apparently she worked wonders on making the family members feel better.

The detectives had interviewed her bosses and work friends, none of them had seen her. But there was one thing they didn't look at.

There was a funeral on that morning.

I knew it was a crazy idea but when I hypothetically planned to get rid of my abusive parents, the idea of stuffing them in another casket certainly came up.

Surprisingly enough it hadn't taken as long as I thought it would to find out where the funeral casket was buried, and as the family were all dead, missing or couldn't care less. There was no opposition to getting a Court Order to get the body dug up.

Well, I say that but that judge I went to. To say he was a stickler for the rules was an understatement. He made sure I tripled checked every single piece of paper before he signed off on it. Ridiculous. Also-

A strong smell of roasting toffee made me smile as I remembered great memories of Halloween with my family. Looking over at the Techs, I cocked my head to see the toffee scanner machine had melted and the Techs were now digging it up.

Why they couldn't just do that from the start I don't know.

As the graveyard filled with the sounds of strawberry lace grass being hacked away and the soft marshmallow ground got dug up. I felt my stomach churn as I started to wonder what it was like for her.

I really didn't want her to be buried alive. I doubt there was a worse way to go, the feeling of choking as she tried to breathe.

No thank you!

I couldn't even start to imagine what it would have been like for Alexis, no one deserved that. No one. Of course I wouldn't know if that was the case until we found her body.

A small part of me hoped I was flat out wrong, I hoped she wasn't in the casket, I hoped she was alive and well after running off somewhere. Maybe she had a reason to run away and not tell anyone where she was.

Of course I knew I was lying to myself. She was dead, that was the sad truth of a few cold cases. Most thankfully involved missing people who turned up decades later, perfectly happy and healthy, I loved those cases.

This wasn't one of those ones though.

"Oh!" someone shouted.

As I looked at the crime scene techs and their little round caramel faces, my eyes narrowed as I saw they were truly shocked, maybe even a little nervous.

Seeing one of them grab a candy floss camera, I walked over to see what all the fuss was about.

After a few seconds I looked down at the brown *wooden* casket. My eyes widened, how the hell had this survived? After the wave was unleashed everyone and everything had turned into a candy or something.

I wanted to climb down and touch it but this wood seemed special, holy almost, this was something beyond strange. Wood was… wood wasn't meant to be a thing now.

"You still want us… to pull it up?" a tall Caramel Tech asked.

I wasn't sure in all honesty. I had never ever been religious but this wood and casket felt holy or something, and who wants to disrupt holy ground?

I forced myself to nod, and the Techs started to pull up the large brown casket whilst one of them filmed it. Partly for evidence, partly for the scientists because they would never believe we had seen real wood, and not from photos.

With the Techs placing the casket on the strawberry lace grass, I started to feel uneasy again. This was the moment, this was the moment I was going to find out if my fears were right.

The Techs started to unscrew the casket and my stomach tightened into the smallest knot possible. I felt physically sick and a headache corkscrewed across my mind for a moment.

I didn't want to know. No one, especially Alex Stormy, should have to be buried alive and suffocate. That was wrong.

But as the Techs popped open the casket, we all gasped and our eyes widened. After a few moments my eyes narrowed on Alexis's smooth skin and her rather beautiful long brown hair. She wasn't a very tall woman so it wouldn't have been difficult to stick her in the casket.

I checked the older man she was buried with and I still couldn't believe it. This was not natural!

Both bodies were made of flesh and blood.

I don't know how these two had survived the wave and being turned into Candy, but they had! My mind tried to understand it all but I just couldn't, and chances are the scientists wouldn't be able to anyway.

Taking a few deep breaths of the… wow. I must have gotten a few whiffs of the casket air because for the first time in years I was breathing in fresh crisp air.

My mouth dropped.

Alexis's hair started to turn into long liquorice laces, her skin turned to gingerbread and her clothes turned to rice paper. My spirit sunk as I felt like I was the one who had killed her.

I knew the Techs were saying something to me but I ignored them. Pain radiated from my stomach as I felt so guilty for making Alexis a candy person. She was fine until I opened the casket, she was fine, she was flesh and blood. But I took that from her.

Forcing those thoughts away, I went to look back at the casket but they were gone as all but one of the Caramel Techs stood there. A tall Caramel man stood there looking at me, he probably needed me to sign some paperwork or something.

"She's being taken to the lab. We'll get the footage to our bosses too, maybe they can understand it. Is that all detective?"

I nodded but his words still hadn't registered with me properly. Then I remembered why my stomach was hurting.

"Was she buried alive?"

It's all I could ask, my mouth, my mind, my soul didn't want to say anything else. I had to know.

The Caramel Tech smiled. "No Detective. There would have been signs if she had. She was already dead,"

Watching the Caramel Tech walk and drive away, I smiled and let out a deep breath as my stomach relaxed. At least I was wrong and she wasn't buried alive.

Knowing that another detective would take over the investigation, I looked around the graveyard, looking at all the unloved and utterly abandoned graves. No one loved these people, no one cared nor looked for them.

I didn't want that for anyone, let alone me so I would do what I always did at the end of a case. I would have a slow walk along the River Thames before working on another case.

As I turned around and started to walk out of the graveyard, being careful not to disturb any of the chocolate headstones, and I relaxed now knowing that justice would be done for Alexis Stormy. And even though she was a candy person, she didn't have to suffer the thing that all candies fear.

AUTHOR OF BETTIE ENGLISH PRIVATE EYE MYSTERIES
CONNOR
WHITELEY
FUTURE BAKING
AN AMATEUR SLEUTH MYSTERY SHORT STORY

FUTURE BAKING

Cheaters will always exist in competitions regardless of whatever the future promises.

The sweet, beautiful aromas of sweet honey boiling away gently on a hob, sweet vanilla cakes cooking slowly in the oven and the gentle rolling boil of homemade jam filled the large white canvas tent that Celebrity Chef Janet Hart was standing in near the front.

This was the first-ever finals of the Great Kent Cook Off and she absolutely couldn't believe that she was finally here, finally getting to judge a cooking show, just like her mother had wanted before she had sadly died of cancer a decade ago.

Janet had to admit that even after ten episodes and ten weekends with all the amazing amateur bakers, the entire setup and tent was still brand-new to her and she was constantly struggling to find where everything was, but she seriously loved this job.

She still enjoyed watching the bakers and cookers chop, slice and mix ingredients like they were babies as they stood behind their tall wooden counter with bright copper ovens (their sponsor's choice, not Janet's) and they were all wearing the custom-made aprons made by yet another sponsor.

The tent was covered in so many blues, reds and whites that she sometimes felt like she was walking into the Union Jack every weekend, but as soon as her co-presenter shouted *Cook* she was in her element.

It was incredible seeing what some bakers were up to these days and trying to combine different combinations of ingredients that Janet had never had the pleasure of eating.

There were three contestants in the final today and Janet was so impressed with them all. Rachel was a typical grandmother baker with long grey hair, pink jumper and she focused on old recipes. Janet wasn't sure if she was going to win but she seemed to be doing enough to impress her and her co-judge.

Robert was another good contestant with his attractive poufy black hair and slim body, who managed amazing flavours every single day but he definitely lacked presentation skills at times. He would never get a job at her restaurants but he was a great guy to be around.

And Sarah was probably the best of all of them if only she could keep her head in the game just long enough to win. Janet admired how driven, strong-willed and bold Sarah was and it almost always paid off but Janet really hoped that she wouldn't make a mistake that would cost her everything.

In fact, Janet was worried about that herself.

Ever since she was a little child she had been watching, studying, learning from cooking shows as much as she could and it was so surreal actually being a judge of her own one but she hated it when her phone buzzed.

Janet took out her brand-new holo-phone that her grandkids had bought her and she managed to unlock the little thing.

And she really hadn't wanted to get an alert from the tent's security equipment showing her that nanobots were present in the tent.

She had never wanted to get the security equipment but the Streaming service had insisted on it with the other claims of cheating on the other cooking programmes and viewers were starting to abandon cooking programmes because of all the cheaters.

Janet understood that, but on her programme she was focusing on how cooking used to be done back in the 2010s and 2020s before the technology of nanobots, robots and all the other methods of cheating got created.

Baking wasn't an art anymore.

A person could simply programme nanobots to create a cake, add them to water and place the water in a hot oven and ten minutes later a person would have a cake that tasted amazing.

That wasn't baking, but hell it was what everyone else was doing. It was why everyone at the streaming service had jumped on Janet's idea for an old-fashioned baking competition.

That was all in doubt now.

Janet looked around for her co-judge and she was laughing in front of the camera after explaining how something worked in baking.

Janet really did love Josephine. She was a smart presenter, very camera friendly and the UK loved her so Janet had no problem asking her for help launching the programme.

And considering that Josephine had been busted with a lot of younger escorts a few months back, she needed to get her career back on track and since it was just an innocent situation made to look bad, Janet was perfectly okay to help out a friend.

It was the least she could do.

As soon as the camera people took their little floating orbs away, Janet went over to her and turned her back to the bakers.

"We have a problem," Janet said, "security system has found nanobots in the tent. I cannot say where they are or who's using them but we have a problem,"

Josephine weakly smiled pointing to the fact that her mic was still on.

Damn it. Janet hadn't even realised that their mics were on all the time during a challenge so the streaming service instantly knew there was a chance cheating was going on.

For the sake of the programme, their future and their careers, Janet had to find out who was using the nanobots and deal with it quietly before this became a national scandal.

And the idea of home, old-fashioned baking was well and truly killed forever.

Janet covered her mic. “How do we find these nanobots? Do they come in a packet or something?”

Josephine shook her head also covering her mic. “I used those nanobots once and they come in a small glass tube with a computer adapter on the end so you can programme them,”

Janet nodded. She didn’t care that Josephine had used them before, part of being a good cook was being able to experiment and get creative.

Janet wiped a drop of sweat off her forehead as the temperature of the tent rose more and more. The challenge they had set the cookers was the very last one of the entire series.

The cookers had to create three different complex desserts and the challenge was about to end in fifteen minutes. That was all the time they had to discover who was using the nanobots.

“So we’re looking for someone having a glass tube in their bin?” Janet asked.

Josephine gave a camerawoman a fake smile as she passed and shook her head. “I don’t know but I doubt it. We could carefully search the bins but what if the criminal has the tube on them?”

Janet shook her head and walked towards the bakers, pretending to be inspecting them decorating their cakes and everything, when she was actually wondering who the hell would risk their reputation and hers over something as stupid as nanobots.

After the past weekends with them, she considered all of them friends so it was just outrageous that they would betray her trust like this.

Janet went over to Robert who was working on making fondant icing for his massive, very-light chocolate mousse cake. It wasn’t exactly as fancy or complex as Janet would have liked but it did look impressive, despite it being out of the fridge when it seriously should have been in one.

Maybe he was the user of the nanobots and that was why he wasn’t putting the cake in the fridge. Maybe he was a cheater.

Janet shook her head and kept walking around the tent, she

managed to look at Robert's bin as she paced but it was empty, completely empty, it was a little weird but not uncommon. The production crew were amazing at their job.

This production crew were far better than she ever was when she was working behind the scenes a few years ago.

Janet went over to the camera people who were crowding around Rachel because she was making spun sugar by making some caramel, flicking it in the air and then the caramel created very thin threads.

It was probably the most advanced thing she had ever tried but she looked like it was going to be placed on top of a Victoria Sponge. Definitely not complex and unless her other two desserts were stunning, there was no chance of her winning.

Janet really wanted to help Rachel by recommending some advanced techniques to at least give her a fighting chance, Rachel was kind and loved her family but Janet couldn't help her.

Hell, even a homemade crème diplomat would help her a great deal and it wasn't even that hard.

As Janet watched the camera people focus their camera orbs on Rachel's "good" side, she just couldn't help but wonder if Rachel was using nanobots to help herself win.

Actually, there was a fairly good chance considering that Rachel worked as a technology engineer during the week, working on massive projects all over England.

Janet frowned as Rachel had said repeatedly how she hated nanobots because they destroyed the art of baking, cooking and creating bread. Janet was sure she was right but that also meant she couldn't be the user.

Unless that had all been an act.

Janet wanted to stomp her feet on the ground. She was a chef, she wasn't a sleuth and she had no idea how to begin to properly investigate this potential crime.

"Five minutes left!" a very tall woman shouted, one of the streaming service's top presenters.

Janet was about to go over to Sarah when she realised that the top presenter actually hated her because the presenter had thought she was some hot-shot baker but Janet had confessed the presenter's biscuits were far worse than her three-year-old grandson's burnt offering the other week.

And that was definitely the truth.

Janet just watched the presenter, called Megan, as she offered words of encouragement, jokes and more to the three remaining bakers and she just knew that Megan was the type of person to sabotage someone's career.

There had been rumours of it for years and Janet had always dismissed them as jealous rumours by people who didn't get the job. Maybe they were right.

"Camera people over here please," Megan said grinning. "I have an announcement and a confession to make,"

Janet looked at Josephine who was studying Sarah's technique for a moment and their eyes locked.

Stop her. Josephine mouthed.

Janet nodded as she quickly picked up Rachel's piping hot mug of tea and she speed-walked over to the camera people.

She kept walking. Getting faster and faster.

She pretended to trip.

Janet threw the boiling hot mug of tea all over Megan just before the camera crew started filming.

They all laughed at Megan and they turned off their camera orbs for a moment as Megan started swearing.

Janet folded her arms and everyone just stopped in the tent as Josephine also came over.

"You know this show is a fraud. All these bakers are using nanobots. I'll destroy you all," Megan said.

Janet shook her head. "You forget dear Megan, the crew have stopped filming, your mic is destroyed and of course the streaming service has all our audio data. They will destroy it and you used the nanobots anyway,"

Megan spat at Janet. "You righteous cow. I am the best baker in the UK and I'll prove it to you,"

Janet couldn't help but laugh at the poor silly woman as Megan shook her fist harder and harder in Janet's direction.

"You will never do anything in TV again because there is no proof of the nanobots and everyone in the tent except me signed an NDA so you can never talk about it. And I certainly will not,"

"Security," Josephine said as two women stormed in and dragged Megan from the set.

Janet turned towards the contestants and they were all actually done. They hadn't abused the distraction and used the extra time to finish off their creations, they had simply stuck to the rules like professional bakers and cookers.

And that made Janet damn proud of all of them.

"Places everyone," a man shouted from the camera crew. "We need to film the ending,"

Janet just laughed because showbusiness never ended and she was so excited about tasting all these delightful creations with her favourite co-judge at her side.

***

The next few hours had been just amazing, Janet was really impressed with how Rachel had created some perfectly executed classics just like how Janet's mother used to make. Including a perfectly done Victoria Sponge, Sticky Toffee Pudding and a sensationally sweet and fruit jam tart, but it just wasn't that creative.

Janet was also seriously impressed with Robert because his flavours were just incredible and she had no idea before now that chocolate, coffee and some strange spice from India she had no idea how to pronounce actually worked. All of his desserts were immense explosions of flavour on the tongue, but it was just a shame that his souffle had dropped just a centimetre.

That just wasn't good enough for Janet. Of course Josephine had tried to convince her that one single centimetre was being too strict and without nanobots it was impossible to stop a souffle from falling, but Janet had managed without it.

It had hardly been a surprise to her and Josephine that Sarah had won by creating three professional-level French desserts that deserved to be in a top-level patisserie and Janet wasn't even sure she could manage some of those crisp, sweet, stunning desserts but no one needed to know that for sure.

So after all the chaos of the past few weeks, the cheating and Megan getting blacklisted from the TV industry forever, Janet was so looking forward to going back to her own cafes and restaurants and kitchens so she could do what she absolutely loved.

She loved baking and cooking and creating brand-new things to add such joy to people's lives that she knew she was never going to give it up. And she was looking forward to the next season of her programme because she realised now she wasn't just a judge on some random cooking show, she was actually protecting the future of baking by making people want to do it once more.

And that was truly a great thing to protect. Something she would happily do until the day she died.

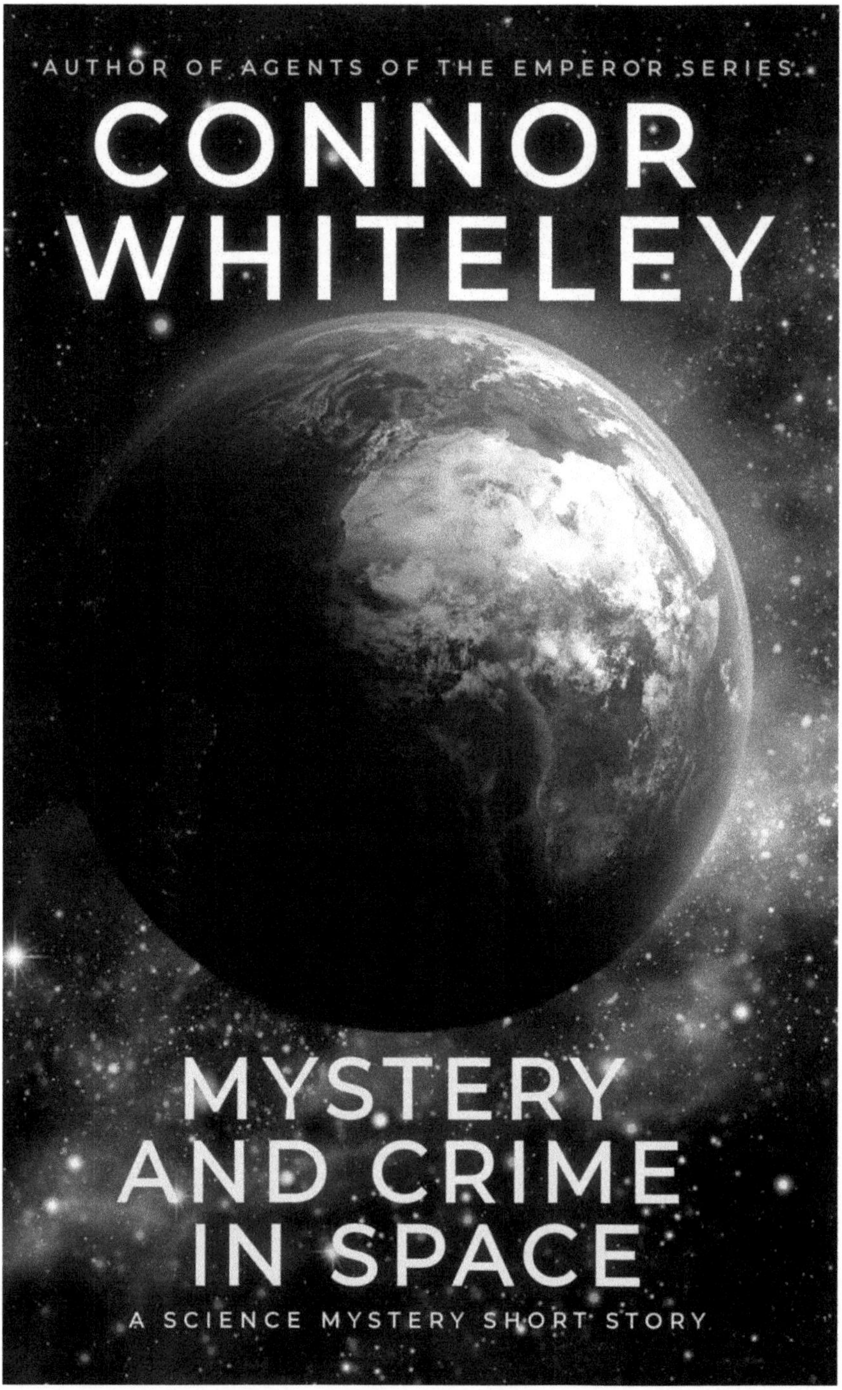
AUTHOR OF AGENTS OF THE EMPEROR SERIES
CONNOR WHITELEY
MYSTERY AND CRIME IN SPACE
A SCIENCE MYSTERY SHORT STORY

MYSTERY AND CRIME IN SPACE

18th August 2022

London, England, Earth

Before Scientist Michael Green fell unconscious and before he had been injected with an unknown substance and before he learnt that the entire galaxy was *deeply* disturbing and mysterious, Michael simply left his little townhouse in the middle of central London and went out down the long curving street with little yellow townhouses lining the street, to get some milk, bread and butter.

Not that Michael knew whatsoever but each one of his steps thundered through time and space and all of creation as people were searching for him, and they wouldn't rest until they had a mere human called Michael Green.

Michael had always loved walking through the wonderful streets of London, now he was entering the busier parts of central London with massive skyscrapers that rose so high into the sky that they seemed to be stabbing the night-time sky itself. The sky above was so peaceful, bright and the entire stars shone in utter defiance against the light pollution of London to create the most stunning starry ocean that Michael had ever seen.

But whilst the sky above might have seen so peaceful, perfect and wonderous, Michael was just a little disappointed at the ground-level. As streams of people went up and down the busy London streets dodging cars, delivery vans and taxis, they were all too busy too see the beauty of the night sky.

Most of them were far too busy focusing on their friends, their phones or even the formidable light-up signs from the different technological companies that warred for customers and London was their battlefield and larger warzone where the fate of companies could be decided. Michael had never paid too much attention to the formidable evil signs before but for some reason he just felt the need tonight.

Michael continued on walking along the busy London streets trying not to get swept up into the current and tide and streams of people hurrying about on their busy nights out. But Michael had time.

Even though all of London seemed to be the exact same area it was so strange how tonight there seemed to be a subtle wind coming from multiple directions. Trying to pull him in one direction or another, but Michael just stayed true to his path, he had to get to the little shop so he could get his vital supplies for his sandwiches tomorrow.

As Michael neared the little shop that was housed inside a bright sterile white former-townhouse on the corner of a busy street that led towards the more touristic areas of London, the air thickened with the delightful aromas of freshly baked pizza, melted cheese and the most amazing caramel that Michael had ever smelt.

He definitely needed to go into the Italian restaurant next to the little corner shop.

Michael was about to enter the narrow doorway to the little shop when his phone fell out of his jeans and smashed onto the floor. Michael just rolled his eyes as he picked up his smartphone and saw that the entire screen was shattered.

That was not what he needed, especially as he wouldn't get paid for another two weeks.

A sharp pain radiated from Michael's neck.

His world went dark.

***

18th August 2022

Unknown Location, *Milky Way Galaxy?*

Michael had absolutely no idea what had happened when his eyes opened, and he was absolutely furious that his neck felt like he was being stabbed repeatedly. It was just his luck that this would matter to him, he couldn't even see anything in front of him the room was so dark.

Michael tried to stand up, only then realising that he was sitting down on something soft, warm and rather comfortable, but something chomped (well felt like) onto his wrists, and Michael hissed. Clearly something was tied around his wrists and when he tried to move his ankles he couldn't move them either.

He was completely trapped.

That was just even more ridiculous and flat out stupid. He was a scientist, a hard worker and he was one to get kidnapped or something.

Michael tried to take some deep breaths to calm down but that only caused more outrageous questions, as he smelt the hints of burnt ozone, slightly cooked flesh and even some lemons. Michael had smelt all of that before in his lab working for the UK Ministry of Defence, more specifically the Space Division that no one knew about.

Maybe that was it, maybe someone from work had kidnapped him as a joke. That would make a lot of sense, maybe it was the jerk newbie Dom he was always pranking people.

A very quiet hum, pop and bang echoed around the room Michael couldn't see in as Michael heard something mechanical move, like an electric garage door opening, and slowly bright streams of light shone through some kind of floor-to-ceiling window.

Michael was so glad to see some light. Ever since he had joined the Ministry of Defence, he had been completely terrified of some foreign power kidnapping him and interrogating him to learn about the "Mighty UK's" space programme. The joke was on them in that space, the UK was pathetic as hell.

Michael focused on what he saw through the window and his mouth dropped and his stomach twisted into a painful knot.

It was flat out impossible but Michael was staring down at Earth, and all around the window were the bright shining stars that had looked so peaceful earlier, but they weren't stars.

They were star-shaped warships.

Michael had never seen anything like that but they were perfectly star-shaped and if Michael had to guess, he predicted that someone who knew a lot about light travelling through space could probably create something to make these warships look identical to stars from Earth.

This was just amazing and terrifying.

The only reason why Michael knew that they were warships was because of the immense cannon attached to the side of each one.

"Doctor Michael Green," someone said.

Michael cocked his head, he never used his doctor title and he didn't tell anyone about it, so how did this person know about it?

That made Michael focus on what was actually important at this moment, so he really forced his eyes away from the stunning, if not terrifying, view out the window and he focused on the room he was contained in.

Michael wasn't exactly impressed with its awful dark grey walls that were perfectly smooth, ceiling that had a number of vents built-in and the floor seemed to have a number of holes in them for some purpose.

White gas shot out of a vent on the far side.

Michael coughed. His throat felt like it was burning.

It was so hard to believe that gas released from a vent on the other side of the room had caused him to feel like this but they had.

He was in massive trouble.

"I am sorry for this Englishman," the voice said again.

For some reason it sounded clearer this time even though it was clearly being projected into the room by a speaker, but Michael couldn't help but detect a faint Chinese accent.

"Chinese?" Michael asked.

The voice laughed. "Of course Englishman,"

Michael forced himself not to panic. This had to be some sort of Chinese spying operation, this was not what he wanted in the slightest. He was surely going to die.

"What's Operation Alpharuis?" the Chinese asked.

Michael smiled to himself that was a fake operation that the UK government had leaked to make their enemies focus on that instead of the real operations going on (that were fruitless at this point), but Michael was much more interested in what actually bound his hands together.

From the light projected from the warships the bonds seemed to be some kind of plastic that created its own warmth and it almost felt alive to some extent. Michael didn't know why he felt that, but he did.

A vent opened. More gas shot out.

Michael coughed. His throat burnt. A trickle of blood ran down his nose.

"My question," the Chinese asked.

"Why are you doing this?" Michael asked. "What the hell is this place?"

"Let me show you little Englishman,"

Michael heard the ceiling hum alive. Needles shot down. Thrusting themselves into his neck.

Michael's world went black.

***

18th August 2022

Chinese Warship, Earth Orbit

Michael was really starting to hate these stupid, pathetic Chinese spies or whatever they were. They were some of the most evil people Michael had ever had the "privilege" of meeting.

A few minutes later Michael found himself laying on an icy cold white floor in the middle of somewhere filled with talking, shouting and barking of orders of somewhere becoming a hive of activity.

Michael forced himself up and he was rather shocked to see himself in a large oval chamber with three rows of Chinese people working at computers above the centre of the oval that Michael was standing in.

Everyone in what Michael could only describe as a bridge was so focused that Michael was almost concerned about what was going on, there was tons of orders being shouted about, results of scans and everything else, Michael was now really glad he had taken Chinese lessons at school.

Michael was about to say something when he noticed five very official looking people standing in front of holograms and an immense floor-to-ceiling window with something on the far side of Earth circled.

Almost like it was being tracked.

"What is this?" Michael asked in perfect mandarin.

The entire bridge stopped and looked at him, they clearly hadn't known of his ability to speak their language.

The youngest of the five officials bowed her respects to the others and came towards Michael. Just out of sheer politeness and a willingness not to die, Michael bowed his respects to her. She seemed impressed.

"What you are looking at Doctor is the future of China-America?" the woman said.

Michael felt his stomach tense. He had heard of this war going on for ages. It was the war between America and China for information, economical superiority and the eternal fight between democracy and autocracy. A war that Michael knew, from hot sexy dinners with his ex-girlfriend, America was badly losing in recent years.

"But you're already winning the war? You're getting more powerful than the US and we all know that you'll be the most powerful economy in the world in the next decade," Michael said.

Of course Michael wished, wanted, needed that to be completely false. He never wanted to live in a world where abominable China was the most powerful country. Michael might not have agreed with everything the Americans did in the few past months, but America was needed, and not all Americans were bad people.

The young Chinese woman gestured Michael to follow her towards the floor-to-ceiling window.

"You aren't wrong," the woman said. "America is a dying country and we will rise with their destruction, but America is dying by a thousand cuts and each American ripping apart the other political side. Killing themselves in the process. We need them to die with a single strike,"

Michael could only nod to hide his utter horror.

"You cannot do that. You don't need to. And come on, how the hell am I standing on a warship in space?" Michael asked.

The young woman smiled as she looked out over the massive starry ocean and stunning planet Earth below.

"The Chinese are never stupid. We developed spaceships in the early 2000s whilst Americans and Europeans and whatever is left of the *United* Kingdom was still playing politics with each other. We rule space,"

"Enemy warships incoming!" someone shouted.

Michael just smiled at the young woman. "You were saying,"

Michael simply looked at the holograms in front of him as he noticed that there were about twenty "enemy" warships incoming from the other side of Earth.

They were American.

Michael had never ever known that the Americans owned spaceships. It was impossible, but clearly the UK was more behind than he feared.

But one fact that was crystal clear was Michael was probably one of the only people able to stop the Chinese from destroying America. He had to save them and by saving America he would save the entire western world.

And billions of lives.

"Americans incoming," the young woman said, "Nova cannons charging. Launch when in range,"

Michael might not have known what a nova cannon actually was, but he knew it was deadly. A supernova was the explosion of a dead star and that engulfed an entire solar system, if the stupid Chinese had developed something of that sort of concentrated power then Michael had to stop it no matter what.

Two hands wrapped round Michael's throat. They spun him around. Pinning him against the icy cold window.

The Chinese man kept squeezing. He was choking Michael.

Michael kicked, punched, tried to scream. He couldn't. The man was too strong.

The man's head exploded.

The young woman stood behind the man as his corpse dropped and she put her gun away, looking almost sorry for Michael.

"My apologises," she said. "He lost his family to British forces so killing you was… revenge,"

Michael just nodded as the young woman went back to work. These Chinese idiots were all crazy, he had to do something.

Michael returned his attention to the holograms and they might have all been in Chinese but he could read them. They were all streams of incoming data about the speed, strength and number of the incoming American ships.

It was crystal clear from the data coming in that the Chinese were delusional about their so-called superiority. All the data was telling him that the Americans outgunned and had stronger shields than the Chinese.

But the American space-weapons didn't have the range the Chinese ships did.

All Michael had to do was make sure the Chinese couldn't fire until the Americans were in range.

That was going to be damn well impossible but Michael had to try.

Michael clicked on a hologram as a data stream containing the location and distance of the American ships changed a little. The

Americans were picking up speed, but Michael tapped a few times and changed the data to show they were slowing down.

Hopefully no one in the Chinese fleet would check them so the Americans would be closer than the Chinese realised.

The data stream deleted Michael's data and he felt the cold metal barrel of a gun against his head.

Michael slowly turned around and just frowned at the young Chinese woman who was pointing the gun at him. Michael looked around at the other Chinese people on the bridge and Michael realised she was the only one with a gun.

"On your knees," she said coldly.

Michael shook his head. He subtly took a step back and started randomly tapping and hopefully typing in words and commands into the holograms.

Red flashing lights exploded on overhead. Gas exploded out of the ceiling.

The young woman looked up. Michael charged forward. His throat burned.

Tackling her to the ground. He punched her. Grabbed the gun.

She kicked him in the nuts. He fell to the ground. She took back the gun.

She pressed it into Michael's mouth.

Michael grabbed her face. He pressed his fingers into her eyes. Rich red blood poured out.

The young woman screamed in agony before her eyeless corpse slumped onto the ground next to him.

Michael couldn't react. He jumped up and picked up the gun.

He aimed it at the four other officials but it was useless. He had to save the American fleet.

Michael aimed the gun at the floor-to-ceiling window.

Chinese men ran at him. He fired.

Bullets smashed into the window. It cracked.

He emptied the gun. The window was only cracked.

Men tackled Michael to the ground. He screamed.

He struggled. He forced an arm free.

Michael threw the gun at the window. Smashing into it.

The window shattered. The entire oval bridge was exposed to the cold deadly vacuum of space.

***

18th August 2022
London, England, Earth

Michael found himself simply leaning against the icy cold brick of a yellow London Townhouse on a deadly quiet street with no other people about, no sounds to slice through the silence and no smells to form on his tongue.

The entire street was perfectly lit with the typically ugly domed street lamps that lit up London each night, and Michael just stood completely unsure of what had just happened.

The entire experience was definitely real, of that he had absolutely no doubt, he had been on a Chinese warship, almost been shot and choked to death and just hoped beyond hope that he had saved the Americans from certain annihilation.

Michael looked up at the peaceful night sky above and just wondered if what he was seeing was actually real. The starry ocean seemed so peaceful, just and perfect like it was something that Earth would aspire to represent, but just couldn't help but wonder if it was all a lie, for how many of those stars were real and how many were actual warships from each side of China-America?

"Thank you Doctor Green," a man said standing next to him with a slight American accent.

If Michael hadn't just been up into space, he might have wondered how the hell an American had appeared next to him, but that really seemed like the most logical part of his evening.

"Did I save you?" Michael asked. It was only then that he realised how badly he hadn't wanted anyone to die.

The man nodded and Michael realised that the man seemed completely engulfed in shadows and shrouded in the darkness of space, even though there was a streetlamp right above them.

"Will I remember tonight?" Michael asked.

The American simply laughed and Michael took that as a maybe.

"Just know Doctor," the man said, "you bought us enough time to get within striking distance and one of our spies on the Chinese ship alerted us to your presence,"

Michael folded his arms. "So when I shattered the window you what… launched a tractor beam to save me?"

"Of course," the American said. "And it isn't a tractor beam, that's science fiction rubbish, we created an oxygen corridor for you and manipulated the air currents to bring you to our ship then we knocked you out and placed you here,"

Michael just nodded. He didn't know if that was better or worse than what the Chinese had done.

The Americans turned to Michael and even though Michael couldn't see his face clearly, he knew he was smiling at him.

"Thank you for everything Doctor. Your shot did stop the Chinese war fleet from attacking us and you did save Earth today. The US will always be grateful to you," the American said before he disappeared.

Michael was just glad he could help and he actually felt amazing.

A chill ran down Michael's back and he looked at his watch. He flat out couldn't believe he had been out for over three hours and he still hadn't gotten his bread, milk and butter.

Michael had no idea what the hell he had been doing for all those hours, but he felt great for some reason and now he had a true mission. He had to get his ingredients for his sandwiches tomorrow because his job was amazing, his life was wonderful and Michael just felt more amazing than any man deserved to feel.

But he just couldn't remember for the life of him what had happened in the past three hours, and it felt important.

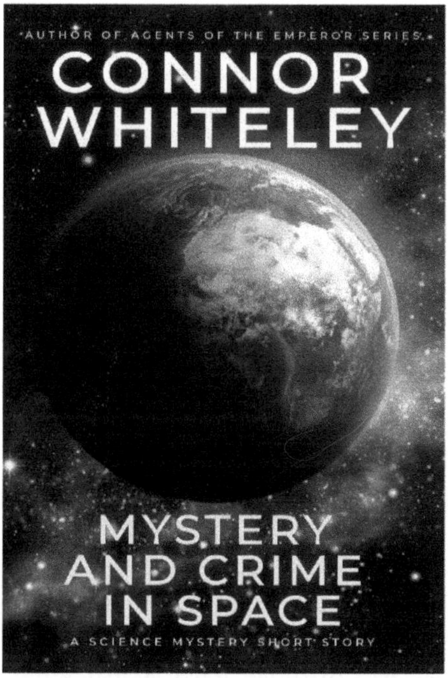

GET YOUR FREE SHORT STORY NOW! And get signed up to Connor Whiteley's newsletter to hear about new gripping books, offers and exciting projects. (You'll never be sent spam)

https://www.subscribepage.io/garrosignup

About the author:

Connor Whiteley is the author of over 60 books in the sci-fi fantasy, nonfiction psychology and books for writer's genre and he is a Human Branding Speaker and Consultant.

He is a passionate warhammer 40,000 reader, psychology student and author.

Who narrates his own audiobooks and he hosts The Psychology World Podcast.

All whilst studying Psychology at the University of Kent, England.

Also, he was a former Explorer Scout where he gave a speech to the Maltese President in August 2018 and he attended Prince Charles' 70th Birthday Party at Buckingham Palace in May 2018.

Plus, he is a self-confessed coffee lover!

Other books by Connor Whiteley:

Bettie English Private Eye Series

A Very Private Woman
The Russian Case
A Very Urgent Matter
A Case Most Personal
Trains, Scots and Private Eyes
The Federation Protects
Cops, Robbers and Private Eyes
Just Ask Bettie English
An Inheritance To Die For
The Death of Graham Adams
Bearing Witness
The Twelve
The Wrong Body
The Assassination Of Bettie English
Wining And Dying
Eight Hours
Uniformed Cabal
A Case Most Christmas

Gay Romance Novellas

Breaking, Nursing, Repairing A Broken Heart
Jacob And Daniel
Fallen For A Lie
Spying And Weddings
Clean Break
Awakening Love
Meeting A Country Man
Loving Prime Minister
Snowed In Love
Never Been Kissed

Love Betrays You
Love And Hurt

Lord of War Origin Trilogy:
Not Scared Of The Dark
Madness
Burn Them All

Way Of The Odyssey
Odyssey of Rebirth
Convergence of Odysseys
Odyssey Of Hope
Odyssey of Enlightment

Lady Tano Fantasy Adventure Stories
Betrayal
Murder
Annihilation

Agents of The Emperor
Deceitful Terra
Blood And Wrath
Infiltration
Fuel To The Fire
Return of The Ancient Ones
Vigilance
Angels of Fire
Kingmaker
The Eight
The Lost Generation
Hunt
Emperor's Council

Speaker of Treachery
Birth Of The Empire
Terraforma
Spaceguard

The Rising Augusta Fantasy Adventure Series
Rise To Power
Rising Walls
Rising Force
Rising Realm

The Fireheart Fantasy Series
Heart of Fire
Heart of Lies
Heart of Prophecy
Heart of Bones
Heart of Fate

City of Assassins (Urban Fantasy)
City of Death
City of Martyrs
City of Pleasure
City of Power

Lord Of War Trilogy (Agents of The Emperor)
Not Scared Of The Dark
Madness
Burn It All Down

Miscellaneous:
Dead Names
RETURN
FREEDOM
SALVATION
Reflection of Mount Flame
The Masked One
The Great Deer
English Independence

OTHER SHORT STORIES BY CONNOR WHITELEY

Mystery Short Story Collections
Criminally Good Stories Volume 1: 20 Detective Mystery Short Stories
Criminally Good Stories Volume 2: 20 Private Investigator Short Stories
Criminally Good Stories Volume 3: 20 Crime Fiction Short Stories
Criminally Good Stories Volume 4: 20 Science Fiction and Fantasy Mystery Short Stories
Criminally Good Stories Volume 5: 20 Romantic Suspense Short Stories

Connor Whiteley Starter Collections:
Agents of The Emperor Starter Collection
Bettie English Starter Collection
Matilda Plum Starter Collection
Gay Romance Starter Collection
Way Of The Odyssey Starter Collection
Kendra Detective Fiction Starter Collection

Science Fiction Short Story Collections

Rivetingly Great Stories Volume 1
Rivetingly Great Stories Volume 2
Rivetingly Great Stories Volume 3
Rivetingly Great Stories Volume 4
Rivetingly Great Stories Volume 5

Mystery Short Stories:

Protecting The Woman She Hated
Finding A Royal Friend
Our Woman In Paris
Corrupt Driving
A Prime Assassination
Jubilee Thief
Jubilee, Terror, Celebrations
Negative Jubilation
Ghostly Jubilation
Killing For Womenkind
A Snowy Death
Miracle Of Death
A Spy In Rome
The 12:30 To St Pancreas
A Country In Trouble
A Smokey Way To Go
A Spicy Way To GO
A Marketing Way To Go
A Missing Way To Go
A Showering Way To Go
Poison In The Candy Cane
Kendra Detective Mystery Collection Volume 1
Kendra Detective Mystery Collection Volume 2
Mystery Short Story Collection Volume 1

Mystery Short Story Collection Volume 2
Criminal Performance
Candy Detectives
Key To Birth In The Past

Science Fiction Short Stories:
Their Brave New World
Gummy Bear Detective
The Candy Detective
What Candies Fear
The Blurred Image
Shattered Legions
The First Rememberer
Life of A Rememberer
System of Wonder
Lifesaver
Remarkable Way She Died
The Interrogation of Annabella Stormic

Fantasy Short Stories:
City of Snow
City of Light
City of Vengeance
Dragons, Goats and Kingdom
Smog The Pathetic Dragon
Don't Go In The Shed
The Tomato Saver
The Remarkable Way She Died
Dragon Coins
Dragon Tea
Dragon Rider

All books in 'An Introductory Series':
Introduction To Psychotherapies
I Am Not A Victim, I Am A Survivor
Breaking The Silence
Healing As A Survivor
Clinical Psychology and Transgender Clients
Clinical Psychology
Moral Psychology
Myths About Clinical Psychology
401 Statistics Questions For Psychology Students
Careers In Psychology
Psychology of Suicide
Dementia Psychology
Clinical Psychology Reflections Volume 4
Forensic Psychology of Terrorism And Hostage-Taking
Forensic Psychology of False Allegations
Year In Psychology
CBT For Anxiety
CBT For Depression
Applied Psychology
BIOLOGICAL PSYCHOLOGY 3RD EDITION
COGNITIVE PSYCHOLOGY THIRD EDITION
SOCIAL PSYCHOLOGY- 3RD EDITION
ABNORMAL PSYCHOLOGY 3RD EDITION
PSYCHOLOGY OF RELATIONSHIPS- 3RD EDITION
DEVELOPMENTAL PSYCHOLOGY 3RD EDITION
HEALTH PSYCHOLOGY
RESEARCH IN PSYCHOLOGY
A GUIDE TO MENTAL HEALTH AND TREATMENT AROUND THE WORLD- A GLOBAL LOOK AT DEPRESSION
FORENSIC PSYCHOLOGY

THE FORENSIC PSYCHOLOGY OF THEFT, BURGLARY AND OTHER CRIMES AGAINST PROPERTY
CRIMINAL PROFILING: A FORENSIC PSYCHOLOGY GUIDE TO FBI PROFILING AND GEOGRAPHICAL AND STATISTICAL PROFILING.
CLINICAL PSYCHOLOGY
FORMULATION IN PSYCHOTHERAPY
PERSONALITY PSYCHOLOGY AND INDIVIDUAL DIFFERENCES
CLINICAL PSYCHOLOGY REFLECTIONS VOLUME 1
CLINICAL PSYCHOLOGY REFLECTIONS VOLUME 2
Clinical Psychology Reflections Volume 3
CULT PSYCHOLOGY
Police Psychology

A Psychology Student's Guide To University
How Does University Work?
A Student's Guide To University And Learning
University Mental Health and Mindset

www.ingramcontent.com/pod-product-compliance
Ingram Content Group UK Ltd.
Pitfield, Milton Keynes, MK11 3LW, UK
UKHW022322190325
456501UK00007B/59

9 781917 722261